Lucky in Love

Port Provident: Holiday Hearts

Kristen Ethridge

I0544398

Dear Reader

JUST ABOUT A YEAR AGO—BEFORE the whole world as we knew it came to a screeching halt—I took a trip for my job out to Las Vegas. I was working behind the scenes at the company's annual leadership and sales kickoff meeting. But because my role was completely under the radar, I had some extra time to see the sights.

I ate in all the best restaurants Mandalay Bay had to offer. I checked out the pool (even though nothing much was going on there in the dead of winter), I rode the gondolas at the Venetian, I sat in jaw-dropping awe as I watched One, the Cirque du Soleil tribute to Michael Jackson, and I put my face on M&Ms to take home to my kids (mom of the year right here—what kid doesn't want a souvenir with mom's face all over it?)

And as I dined on risotto and sampled bread pudding and saw the sights, a book came together.

All the best books are inspired by real life. Or at least I think mine are. I love taking something that's everyday real and making it sparkle and shine through the lens of fiction.

And I loved getting to spend more time with Lisa Fleming. You met her in The Cupid Caper—and now she's back and getting her own chance at love. I think you will love Lisa and Ryan—and Nana and Pops. There's a lot going on here, and it all comes together with a touch of kismet that only a place as over-the-top as Las Vegas can bring.

(But don't worry...you'll still get to spend some time in Port Provident too!)

Here's to the adventures we've all been holding in our hearts for the past year while the world's been on pause. May the doors to our world open back up soon—and until then, may stories like Lisa and Ryan's sweep us away to destinations in our imagination.

All the best-

Kristen

PS... I'D LIKE TO INVITE you to become a part of my reader community today. Just go to www.kristenethridge.com. You'll see the box to join right at the top of the page.

One of my signature Sweet Escape Romances is Layla and Ridge's story, *A Place to Find Love*. Layla's spent her whole life searching for a greater meaning in her life. She comes to Port Provident running on fumes, but once she meets Ridge, she begins a journey that fills her with more than she ever hoped for—faith, family, and a place to find the love she's always longed for. I'll send you a copy just for joining my reader community, plus you'll be able to keep up with the latest on my books and Port Provident through regular emails and more reader bonuses.

I promise these stories will lift you up and leave you with a smile.

One of the best ways to get to know Port Provident even better is to get your *Passport to Port Provident*. It's a behind-the-scenes reader exclusive that's available when you join me on Facebook Messenger[1].

www.kristenethridge.com[2]
Facebook[3] Pinterest[4] Twitter[5] Instagram[6]
The Port Provident Community Center[7]

---

1.   https://m.me/KristenEthridgeBooks

2. http://www.kristenethridge.com

3. https://www.facebook.com/KristenEthridgeBooks

4. http://www.pinterest.com/kethridgebooks/

5. https://twitter.com/kristenethridge

6. https://instagram.com/kristenethridge

7. https://www.facebook.com/groups/2422381554654795

Chapter One

"POPS, THERE'S NO WAY you're convincing me you brought those for the USO lounge."

Ryan McBride nodded his head in the direction of the two dozen roses, wrapped in cellophane and tissue and tied with an oversized crimson-red bow.

Ryan caught a glance at Pops, who looked like he won the Miss America pageant. That explanation seemed just as ridiculous as this last-minute trip to the florist and then the airport—since Ryan knew neither had anything to do with America's heroes. That much was as clear as the plastic sheet surrounding the bouquet.

Bill McBride climbed in the car and sat down, careful not to crush the flowers as he buckled his seatbelt. "I support our troops, Ryan."

"I didn't say you didn't, Pops. I know you do. You've been one of them and had their back ever since." Ryan let his eyes leave the road long enough to give his grandfather a stern stare. "But usually when I take you to the airport to welcome home our troops, you let a 'thank you' and a handshake suffice. And you usually wear your American Legion cap. Not a tie. Pops, don't lie to me. What's going on here?"

Bill stared ahead stoically, seemingly considering his words before he spoke as they made their way down Interstate 15 to McCarron International Airport.

Ryan decided he would just let Pops have the next word. Ryan read the bluffs of others for a living, a very lucrative living.

And he'd just called Pops's bluff. He had Pops, and the old man knew it.

"Well," Pops dragged out the syllable, still unwilling to commit to revealing whatever he had up his starched long sleeve.

"*Mmm-hmm*?"

"You see, I'm meeting someone there." Then he added hastily, "Not a service member, though."

"I figured that one out already, Pops. Keep going." Ryan turned into the main entrance to the airport. "What airline, Pops?"

"American. She's coming from Texas." Pops pointed at the sign just ahead, which directed them to the terminal where American Airlines landed. "Ok, so, keep going. What's her name?"

Pops bent his head low, smelling the flowers, almost as though he was enjoying the perfume worn by his mystery woman.

Ryan snuck another glance at Pops. When had he had time to meet a woman? And especially one from Texas? When Bill had moved to the retirement community a year ago, Ryan half expected him to find companionship over the Friday night bingo cards.

But Texas?

Something wasn't adding up.

Was it possible that Pops wasn't playing with a full deck anymore?

And while Ryan didn't understand the whole situation right now, he did understand odds. And the odds of his ninety-two-year-old grandfather meeting a woman from halfway across the country were virtually non-existent.

"Gina Mae," Pops lowered his voice and ran the syllables together into a mumble. "Her name is Gina Mae Lee. Well, Gina Fleming now. But back when I knew her, she was Gina Mae Lee. And she was something."

A career as a card shark had made Ryan mostly immune to displays of emotion. Emotion got you burned. Emotion opened the door to letting someone take advantage of you.

Emotion was for losers.

"Ok, Pops. Gina Mae Something from Texas is coming to visit. And you got her flowers." Ryan swung into a parking space and put his sports car in park. "Why?"

Pops turned his head toward the window and stared as though he was seeing another time and another place.

"Because she's getting ready to become Mrs. Bill McBride, and every gal deserves something special on her wedding day. Especially my gal."

"Your gal, Pops?" Ryan finally let emotion sneak out in his words. "This is a little ridiculous, don't you think? First, you tell me we're going to greet the troops. Then you come out carrying an entire florist's shop, and now you're marrying some girl with a bunch of names at the airport?"

Ryan couldn't figure out why Pops was trying to deceive him. Their relationship had been built on trust and honesty, for as long as Ryan could remember.

Bill cut off Ryan's questions. "She's not some girl with a bunch of names. She was my first love. And she'll be my last. You've got a cynic's heart. You'll never understand."

Bill placed a defiant hand on the door latch and gave it a strong pull that was more Chuck Norris than Chuck E. Cheese.

"Won't understand? First love, last love, huh? Where does Memaw fit in? Did you forget about the woman you were married to?"

Pops stopped his exit from the car and turned to look right at Ryan. His fluffy white eyebrows lowered like fanciful caterpillars over his ice-blue eyes. "She's been gone since you were four, Ryan. And that's a long time to live with nothing but memories when all you want is a hand to hold. I doubt I have five more years on this earth, youngster. I'm going to make my time count. And that's exactly what she told me to do, for your information."

He put one leg deliberately out of the car, then stood carefully, cradling the riot of red blooms like a newborn baby. "And whether you stay or leave me to call a taxi to take me and my bride back to town, you'll never speak so disrespectfully to me again, young man. Do you hear?"

Ryan took in a slow breath. If he didn't back off, Pops was going to take a cab to a little white chapel.

"I hear you, Pops. I don't get any of this. But I hear you."

"Good. Then let's get going. Gina Mae's never been to Las Vegas. I don't want to make her wait in a crowded airport by herself."

Ryan watched Pops stand a little taller as he walked to the door. He had moved Pops out here to the desert southwest to try and improve his health and quality of life. Sadly, it seemed like nothing had made much of a difference...until this moment.

Ryan followed his grandfather's eager steps through the airport. He scooted around women toting pink rhinestone doggy carriers. He slid past groups of men slapping each other on the back and gearing up for a bachelor party. He ducked out of the way of tall blondes with fake tans and faker female features, the Playboy-cloned girls looking to make it big at some club, some hotel, some limelight.

Everything Ryan saw as they walked made sense to him. They were all part of the biggest stereotypes about Vegas.

The only thing head-scratcher was everything Pops had just told Ryan. He couldn't make sense of how this all happened and Ryan never suspected a thing. Wasn't he supposed to watch for "tells"—those little behaviors that signaled something to come?

Maybe he was losing his touch.

But he would make absolutely sure he wasn't going to lose Pops.

Ryan McBride didn't know a thing about Gina Mae What's-Her-Name. But he knew he'd protect his grandfather from lions, tigers, bears...and gold diggers.

Which was about the only explanation Ryan could come up with for flying halfway across the country and marrying someone you hadn't seen in decades. Every other explanation defied logic. And logic and odds ruled Ryan's life. He always went where the logic led. Let others be led by gut feelings. Ryan McBride hadn't gotten to the top of one of the highest-stakes games in the world by trusting his feelings.

Right now, he didn't trust Pops' feelings, either.

"There she is, son!" Pops raised his arms and waved the flowers furiously over his head. "Gina Mae!"

Ryan saw a diminutive tuft of white hair coming their way. The little walking cotton ball didn't look like much of a threat. But Ryan had seen enough bluffs at the tables to know things weren't always what they seemed.

IF WHAT HAPPENED IN Vegas was supposed to stay in Vegas, then Lisa Fleming wasn't happening.

Because she sure as Cirque du Soleil wasn't staying here.

And neither was Nana. Nana just didn't know it yet.

But since the moment Lisa had come home from her last day of teaching high school before Spring Break and Nana had handed her a plane ticket to Las Vegas, then blurted out a hare-brained scheme that she'd reconnected with her first childhood love on social media, Lisa had felt like she had joined a movie with the National Lampoon's squad about the worst vacation ever.

But, no. That wasn't enough. As soon as the flight attendant served Nana a tiny glass of overpriced wine, Nana had to go and drop the Nana bomb.

She wasn't just going on vacation to see the fountains at the Bellagio or to waste Lisa's inheritance one shiny coin at a time in a nickel slot machine.

Nope, Nana announced she was getting married in a Vegas chapel to her early-days-of-World-War-II sweetheart.

At that moment, Lisa had flagged down the flight attendant and ordered a tiny bottle of whatever the airline was serving. And now, with every step she took through the airport, she wished she'd ordered one for the road. Or the terminal. Or the baggage claim. Or whatever.

Nana was over ninety years old. Lisa couldn't keep her from going on a trip. But somewhere over New Mexico, empowered by that teeny-tiny adult beverage, Lisa decided she *could* keep Nana from making the biggest mistake of her life.

It was completely possible for Nana to go to Vegas and catch up with an old friend.

She just didn't have to marry him, for Pete's sake.

And if that meant giving up a nice, relaxing Spring Break to ensure that Nana, the woman who protected Lisa her whole life, stayed away from little white Vegas wedding chapels—then so be it.

Once safely past small airport lounges filled with cigarette smoke and dreams of jackpots, Nana gained speed. Lisa found herself trying to keep up with Nana's imitation of the Senior Olympics track squad. Then, once she'd cleared baggage claim, Nana sprinted toward a gentleman in a perfectly starched dress shirt and fell straight into his arms as though she had tripped and landed there.

As they stayed locked in a warm embrace, Lisa began to feel as though she were intruding. They were surrounded by strangers and serenaded by the sounds of luggage carousels, but still Lisa like an outsider at this moment that had been more than six decades in the making.

She'd never had a relationship that had been more than six months in the making.

Lisa looked over Nana's shoulder and above the white-haired man's softly bent head.

She couldn't miss the sight of midnight blue eyes, black hair, and a chiseled chin locked in a light dusting of yesterday's beard. Of all the people in this busy airport, the man behind the couple-of-the-moment had caught her attention.

The way he was staring at Nana and her friend made Lisa uncomfortable, like when she watched scary movies and knew something was about to happen just by the music.

"Are you waiting on something?" Lisa could hear the shortness in her own voice come out like the lead housewife on a catty reality show. "You can just get your suitcase and move on, you know."

He narrowed his eyes. "Can't."

"Didn't your mother teach you staring was rude?"

"Nope."

Ugh. Did the man know how to put two syllables together? Lisa's inner diva had reached a fast, bubbly boil. There was nothing she could do to prevent what was about to happen.

"Well, she should have. I can correct that right now, if you'd like."

That was her Grade-A teacher voice. The beast had been unleashed. No going back now. Mr. Annoying needed to get his suitcase and head for the exit.

"Not really."

Well, at least he used more than one syllable. The Grade-A teacher in her appreciated that.

Her eyes unlocked from his and swept downward.

Whoa, diva... Now Lisa's inner teacher was speaking directly to her, reminding her that this was no time to appreciate any of his finer qualities. Not his syllables...or anything else.

He might have been nice to look at, but his manners didn't match his looks. "There are plenty of taxis outside just waiting to take you wherever you need to go. This is a private moment."

Before Mr. Midnight Eyes could reply, the older gentleman pulled two steps back out of the embrace with Nana.

"He can't go get a taxi. He *is* the taxi," Bill said. "Gina Mae, this is my grandson, Ryan McBride."

Ryan tilted his head toward the reunited couple, in a wordless form of greeting.

Cocky jerk. He could have just answered her original question. She'd just used her teacher voice for nothing.

"Well isn't that fun?" A smile came over Nana's face and she gestured back at Lisa. "Bill, this is my great-granddaughter, Lisa Marie."

Ugh. Every time Nana said that, Lisa felt like she was about to be painted on velvet and hung up at Graceland.

Lisa held her palm up and tried to deflect. "Lisa. Lisa will do."

The world was only big enough for one Lisa Marie in a town with an Elvis impersonator in every white chapel on every corner.

Bill McBride walked over to Lisa and picked up her hand. He lifted it and gave a short peck just over the crest of the knuckles. "Pleased to meet you, my dear. Thank you for bringing my Gina Mae safely to me."

The sincerity with which Bill spoke touched Lisa's heart and made her feel a little guilty for having zero intention of abandoning her plan to circumvent this wedding somehow and get back to this airport as quickly as possible in order to go home.

But since her Nana had always been a big believer in the adage that said you get more flies with honey than vinegar, she was willing to be sweet for now. Goodness knows Nana had drilled the concept into Lisa's head over the years.

She packed up the teacher voice.

"If I'd known we were meeting a true gentleman like you, we'd have been here sooner," Lisa said with a smile. Honestly, the groom-to-be held an irresistible charm, like a chivalrous teddy bear.

Nice to know there were men like that in the world. Too bad they were all ninety years old.

Lisa could feel the stare of Bill's grandson from his staked-out spot just a few feet away. *Sooo.* The apple fell pretty far from Bill McBride's gallant tree.

Too bad. Those eyes would have been a perfect complement for chivalry. Wasn't blue the color of something knightly? Lisa couldn't remember the old stories. She left those things to her friends in the English department.

But hey, it wasn't like Lisa had time to flirt anyway.

She needed to save Nana from herself, her crazy plans, her long-suspected memory issues, and one well-mannered teddy bear who was probably in the same synapse-induced twilight that Nana was.

"Shall we go? Ryan, can you grab my sweetheart's bags? Her hands are full." Bill smiled first at Gina Mae and then at the oversized puff of flowers she could barely fully grasp with her arthritic fingers.

"Sure, Pops." Ryan reached behind his grandfather and plucked the handle of Nana's rolling suitcase. "Got it."

Mr. Blue Eyes was a man of few words. Hopefully, his apparent lack of interest meant he wouldn't be in her way the next few days as she brought some balance back to Nana's life.

"You need any help?" Ryan McBride's voice reminded her of caramel. Low, slow, and with just a hint of burnished sweetness. Now that he'd uttered several syllables together, his voice surprised Lisa. After years in the world of the theater, listening for tone and inflection in the spoken word came as second nature. It was just an analysis she made without even really thinking about it.

His candied voice made Lisa's stomach growl a little as it made her blood pressure rise a few notches with the awareness of it.

Lisa shook her head. "I've got it." At least she could confidently say she had one thing under control here.

Nana and Bill took the lead, walking toward the doors that led to the parking lot with the lightness of step most commonly seen in teenagers. Lisa couldn't believe it. Nana had moved in with her two years ago when it became clear that the day-to-day tasks of keeping a house cleaned and maintained, and dinner cooked, and laundry washed were just taking a physical toll on her. But now, here in the middle of Las Vegas, holding hands with her long-lost first love, it seemed like the years had just disappeared—from both the calendar and her arthritic knees.

The transformation amazed Lisa, and she tried to keep herself from looking obviously drop-jawed as she followed the newly reunited couple.

Standing directly behind Ryan McBride forced Lisa to keep her potentially drop-jawed state in check, too.

He wore a plain black T-shirt and a pair of jeans that seemed dyed to match the black-blue of his eyes. The shirt and the jeans both seemed to fit him like a casual second skin, careless yet confident at the same time.

Snap out of it, Lisa Marie. The only thing she needed to be confident of right now was making sure that her Nana escaped Vegas without making decisions she clearly didn't think all the way through. Nana needed help, and Lisa couldn't risk a wrong move by being distracted.

Her toe collided with six inches of brightly-painted concrete that divided two handicapped parking spots. Lisa flailed her left arm a bit, trying to regain balance. Her suitcase landed with a thud as she jerked it over the offending curb.

Quickly, she lifted her chin up to see if anyone noticed.

Ryan raised an eyebrow.

Lisa took a deep breath in through her nose, resisting the challenge. Yep, she had everything under control.

Or not.

But she was darned sure gonna fake it 'til she made it. No one in Las Vegas would notice a little more fake, would they?

WHEN THEY ALL GOT TO the car, Ryan realized immediately he had a big problem on his hands. His fancy European sports car really wasn't made to chauffeur four grown adults, two suitcases, two carry-on bags, two purses, and one oversized bouquet of roses.

He ran a hand through his hair in a swipe of frustration. He loved Pops, but everything about today had been crazy. If Pops had just been honest with him, maybe they could have made plans for transportation with an adequate number of seats and square feet of trunk space. If Pops had come clean from the start, maybe they wouldn't have been in this predicament at all. Because Ryan would have tried every negotiation skill at his disposal to talk Pops out of this craziness.

Which Pops obviously knew, the crafty old man.

And so, that brought Ryan to standing outside a black convertible sports car in a parking garage, wondering how everything—including the accompanying cast of characters—was going to wedge in there.

"Pops? Where are we going? I'm not taking these ladies back to your retirement home, am I?"

"Well, of course not, Ryan. It's not a hotel. I made Gina Mae a reservation at your place. In the honeymoon suite." Pops' eyes lit up with an arctic twinkle.

"At my place? You mean the Renaissance Grand?" The honeymoon suite at the newest and most talked about hotel on the Vegas strip did not come cheap.

Pops nodded as he opened the door. "Yes, sir. I put my girl there because I thought you'd be able to help her if she needed anything. She wasn't sure her great-granddaughter would come, but since she's here now, maybe you can help me with getting her a room too."

"Wait. Don't get in the car yet. I'm not sure how everything's going to fit, Pops." He popped open the trunk and picked up the first suitcase, trying a few different angles to get them to both fit. His game of suitcase Tetris worked, but barely.

With that task completed, Ryan turned his attention back to Pops and the limited space inside the car.

"So, can you help me get another room at your place, Ryan?" Pops leaned over and slid the seat forward, then started to help Gina Mae into the half-sized back seat.

Out of the corner of his eye, Ryan noticed Gina Mae's great-granddaughter standing cautiously to the side. Clearly, she didn't want to get in Pops' way, but she wasn't convinced her assistance was not going to be needed. Ryan recognized the skeptical half-scowl on her face because it was written across his own. He could feel his eyebrows knitted into a quirky furrow.

"Your place?" The skepticism wasn't just pasted on her face. It was woven through her voice too. "Do you own the hotel or something?"

Ryan had lived out under the glittering lights of Vegas long enough to automatically read into that statement. In this world, things were so often not what they seemed. And that included a long-lost girlfriend and her tag-along great-granddaughter.

Ryan hated that "gold digger" popped into his mind immediately. But he'd been trained a long time ago to look for signs and to anticipate the next move and then the next, and the next, so on until he reached the end game.

Why would some Social Security recipient find his grandfather online and drag along her great-granddaughter on this trip? Gina Mae seemed sincere and her great-granddaughter looked a little overwhelmed. But in this stop in the Nevada desert, things just were rarely what they seemed.

Everyone had a story.

And everyone knew that what happened in Vegas stayed in Vegas.

Except for this time. Ryan knew something didn't add up. He knew these two would not be staying in Vegas. They were on the next plane back to Texas, even if he had to charter a flight himself.

"Ryan?" Pops's voice had the bark of a drill sergeant.

"Yeah?" Ryan answered without a thought, still trying to make sense of what was going on.

"The young lady asked you a question. Are you going to reply?"

Pops's tone and words made Ryan feel very small. He hadn't been taken down a notch in a long time. As the winner of the last four consecutive Global Poker Challenge rings, most people in this town knew who Ryan McBride was. And they all treated him with a champion's deference.

"No, it's not my hotel. I just live there." Ryan looked over the convertible top of the car at the woman with the honey-blonde curls that fell over her shoulders and trailed down her back. "Pops? What are you doing?"

Bill ducked his head low and squished like a crab into the narrow back seat of the car.

"Sitting with my sweetheart. Is that okay?"

Ryan pushed his hand through his hair again. He usually carefully controlled all physical signs of emotion, reluctant to ever tip off an opponent. It was a key to playing good poker.

Good thing he was not at a table this afternoon. There was no way he could ever have concealed everything he thought about this whole crazy trip.

"Sure, Pops. I just didn't think you two would fit comfortably back there. I'm not even sure that seat is made to hold preschoolers."

"Well, I wouldn't say it's comfortable, but we'll do." Bill squeezed the hand of the woman next to him and looked into her eyes with a relaxed smile. "Right, Gina Mae?"

Her smile bookended his. "Right as rain, Bill. My flowers are a bit squashed, though. Lisa Marie, get in the car and hold these, will you?"

Ryan saw Lisa exhale sharply. "Sure, Nana. Pass them up."

Lisa ducked and slid into the front seat, then moved it up to give some more room to the cramped passengers in the back seat. She laid the proffered bouquet in her lap. Ryan caught a glimpse of her as he started the car and adjusted the volume on the radio. Between the curly hair, pinned up in a clip at the crown of her head, and the oversized riot of flowers, Lisa looked like an exasperated beauty queen.

In a town where most of the beauty was exactly as the adage said—skin deep—something about Lisa's soft features made Ryan do a brief double-take. He wasn't used to seeing a woman with no makeup and her hair carelessly secured with a plastic clip. For all that he didn't understand why she was here or what her endgame would wind up proving to be, something about her was refreshing.

Ryan mentally slapped himself as he backed out of the parking space. It was never just about the chips your opponent put on the table or the cards they showed.

It was always about the endgame.

And until Ryan McBride knew what Lisa Marie Fleming and her little great-grandmother were up to, then he needed to stay on top of his own game so he and Pops didn't come up with the losing hand.

No mental lapses. No loss of concentration. No signs that gave away his thoughts.

And no second glances at a clean, fresh face framed by some spiral waves of honey and brown sugar.

"MR. MCBRIDE. IT'S GOOD to see you." A uniformed man opened the door as they pulled under the valet porte-cochere at the Renaissance Grand. Another uniformed man materialized at Lisa's door and swung it open, then helped her get out.

What in the name of Velvet Elvis were they wearing? Were those pantaloons?

Lisa narrowed her gaze, studying the strips of red and black and gold fabric fashioned into some kind of bubble shorts.

There were tights.

And feathers in floppy velvet berets.

She was looking at both of the freaking gentlemen of Verona. Good grief. Wait until she told her best friend Amanda—the English teacher back at Port Provident High School who loved all things Shakespeare.

Lisa stood back and looked at everything else surrounding her. Shades of red and gold and black set the tone for the entire entrance. The floor into the main lobby was black marble, polished to a high shine. A red carpet rolled out to the edge of the sidewalk. Lisa walked over to it to wait out of the way of the hustle and bustle. She remembered attending the Tony

Awards years ago, stunned by all the glitter, spotlights, and theater royalty.

That night felt special, otherworldly. She had to admit that the Renaissance Grand felt much the same right now.

This was definitely like no other world she'd ever seen.

She'd been sucked into some parallel-universe-other-dimension-time-warp thing.

But she couldn't lose her focus on the one thing that did make sense: getting Nana on the next possible plane back to Texas.

And while she was at it, Lisa silently thanked the little twinkling stars on the fake Da Vinci-styled ceiling above her that there were no men in velvet berets in Texas.

"Nana? Are you okay?" Lisa called to her great-grandmother, being gently escorted to the red carpet by one of the Veronian-style doormen on one side, and Bill on the other. The uniformed man who'd opened Ryan's door grabbed both of the suitcases effortlessly, and as they neared the valet station, Lisa saw Ryan hold out a small roll of green-and-cream bills as a note of thanks.

"Should we take your car over to the residence's garage, Mr. McBride, or will you be coming back for it soon?" The man with the suitcases reached out, took the tip, and discreetly tucked them in his pocket.

"Go ahead and take her back to my space, Kip. I'm playing in the celebrity lead-up to the charity tournament tonight. It'll be a short walk home."

"Charity tournament?" Ryan's grandfather turned with an emotional reaction. "Ryan, our rehearsal dinner is tonight. You've got to come with us."

Ryan came up alongside his grandfather as Gina Mae hesitated behind them slightly. "Pops, I've been booked to play tonight for months. You've kind of sprung this whole wedding bells scenario on me in just the last hour or so, and I still don't quite understand why you kept this all a secret. Where are you having dinner? What time?"

The gentleman stopped and leaned up against the first black marble pillar just inside the door. "Well, I don't have a place yet. I was hoping you could recommend something. You know all the best places here."

"Pops, I know a lot of great places. And the best are booked well in advance." Ryan looked toward the corner of the room, then continued to follow the man with the suitcases to the reception desk. "Which I might could have helped you with if you'd given me a heads up about your plans."

Bill looked at Ryan and gave him a shrug, then looked down at the floor. "You'd have talked me out of it, Son. I didn't want you calculating the odds," he said, the words almost falling under his breath. Bill waited for Gina Mae to catch up. Once her hand was firmly in his again, they both followed in Ryan's wake.

Lisa trailed behind, feeling no hurry to get checked in. Despite the anachronistic Veronians, the hotel was beautiful. Shiny, bold colors were everywhere. The decoration was impeccable and modern yet with a strong Italian Renaissance feel.

Every tell-tale sign pointed to the fact that this wasn't a place she'd choose to stay on a teacher's salary. She'd have to figure out which almost-maxed-out credit card to put the next few days on. Lisa thought about the air conditioner repair her car needed and mentally moved it back several months on the calendar. Summer in Texas without A/C in her car was going to stink—literally—she'd be a sweating mess—but getting Nana out of here safely came before any creature comforts.

Even though Lisa wished she could find an online coupon and book the smallest room this place offered, as best she could figure out from the conversation between Ryan and the valet, Ryan lived somewhere nearby. He'd said he was playing in a tournament tonight. Surely he didn't afford a residence in all this luxury by gambling?

Based on what he'd said back at the airport, it was more likely that he had some kind of ownership share in this hotel or something equally out of Lisa's orbit.

Whatever he did, Ryan McBride clearly did it well.

Because Lisa was not at Port Provident High School anymore. This was a world of glitz she'd only heard of from others. And she was pretty sure everything about Ryan McBride and Las Vegas was way, way out of her league.

And Nana's too.

Everything in this lobby strengthened Lisa's resolve to get Nana out of this mess and get her the help she needed to make sure she was living out the rest of her years comfortably. Nana had practically raised her and had supported Lisa's long-dimmed Broadway dreams. She deserved to have Lisa looking out for her now. The tables had turned, and it was Lisa's obligation—no, privilege—to take care of the one person who'd never let her down.

Lisa looked at Nana, gently supported by Bill as they caught up to Ryan at the front desk. The older gentleman seemed sincere. And the look on his face at the airport when he took Nana into his arms had been just precious.

But that didn't mean the plans Nana and Bill had apparently made were in either of their best interests.

Nana had always looked out for what was best for Lisa. She'd given sound counsel and wise advice through the years. Lisa could do no less for Nana now.

"We've got everything taken care of, Mr. McBride. You know we'll always do what we can for you, sir."

Lisa made it to the counter in time to watch Ryan place a black American Express Centurion card on the marble countertop. The onyx plastic blended almost perfectly with the surface on which it had been so casually laid.

AmEx Black. Wow. She'd heard about them, but never actually seen one. She didn't play in that league, herself—a charge card given by invitation only, to people with eight figures of net worth and an annual income of more than a million dollars a year.

Quickly, she revised her estimation of Ryan McBride's league.

She wasn't just way, way out of it. She was *way, way, way* out of it.

Like millions upon millions of ways out of it.

"So, we'll be at the Gran Mona Lisa at six-thirty, Russell. That will give my grandfather and his bride here enough time to dine and I can still be at the celebrity thing for the charity tournament by nine-thirty." Ryan tucked the sleek rectangle of black plastic back in his wallet after the man behind the counter swiped it.

Lisa wondered if his wallet would slide back in those form-fitting jeans easily and caught herself staring just a little too long at some of Ryan McBride's more valuable assets in front of her.

She blew out a harsh breath through pursed lips, mentally chiding herself for thinking more about Ryan McBride than her mission to protect Nana. She only had a matter of days to get this straightened out and get Nana on a plane back home—and booked in for a follow-up with the dementia specialist—without a wedding ring in tow.

"Lisa Marie? Are you okay?" Nana's voice brought Lisa back to the here and now.

"Sure, Nana. Just a long day, that's all. Some of us have been up since five-thirty this morning, in another time zone."

"Well, it's five o'clock now," Bill said. "Why don't you ladies go get some rest and get freshened up. We'll meet you at the restaurant for dinner. What floor is it on, Ryan?"

"Fourth. Where are you going until dinner, Pops?"

"I thought I could go back to your place."

Ryan shrugged. "Sure, but it's kind of a long way over to the residence tower. I may live at the Renaissance Grand, but where I live isn't the same as the hotel. I can get one of the guys to get you a golf cart to shuttle you over there."

"I'll be fine, fine." Bill seemed so sure of himself. "And you two, will you be fine?"

Gina Mae absently patted the bottom of her silver curls. "Yes, of course. This is a lovely place."

"What about you, Lisa?"

It was sweet that Bill was so concerned about his guests.

"Well, one question. What's the dress code at this place? Nana packed—I have no idea what's even in this suitcase."

Bill twitched his lip into a thoughtful half-frown. "Well, I don't know. Ryan?"

"For women, cocktail dresses or higher." His eyes looked down and his gaze came to rest on the toes of Lisa's bright yellow sneakers. "The Mona Lisa is the nicest restaurant on the property."

Nana shook her head. "I brought my bright blue dress. I can wear that. But I didn't pack anything fancy like that for you. I just brought that dress you wore to the winter formal at school. I thought it would match the flowers I want for the wedding. I want a big bouquet of roses."

"Is there a place that sells dresses here?" Lisa swallowed, thinking about what kind of shops—and price tags—would be in an ostentatious palace like this.

Her poor credit card. Her poor, plain old green American Express card that was almost to the limit.

Ryan pointed toward the opening to a long, wide hall. "There are shops over there. Look, I'll get Charley to take care of your Nana and my Pops and I'll show you. I need to check on a few things for tonight and the shops are on my way to the elevators."

Lisa hated shopping. Then, she rolled her eyes back in her head as she thought of something she hated even more.

Shopping on a tight deadline.

And an even tighter budget.

In a hotel that clearly didn't know the first thing about affordable.

Especially schoolteacher affordable.

Just one more thing she now needed to sort out, thanks to Nana and her crazy ideas. So far Spring Break was anything but the relaxing time Lisa had planned on.

"IT'LL WORK."

Chapter Two

"YOU READY FOR TONIGHT, Lucky Charm?" Mariela Donaldson, the manager of the Rosé Boutique, called as they walked in.

Ryan smiled at the striking silver-headed woman behind the ornate counter at the back. She'd managed this shop for a decade, and this wasn't exactly his first visit with a woman that he was trying to impress. Except this time, he wasn't worried about impressing Lisa—just taking care of business. But he didn't have time to tip off Mariela. And on top of that, explaining his true feelings about today's whole mess would simply come across as rude. He decided just to stick to poker talk. "The fun doesn't really begin until tomorrow."

"Then what are you doing in here?"

Ryan turned and looked for Lisa, who hadn't made it more than two steps inside the door. "Mariela, meet Lisa Fleming. Lisa, you'll be in good hands with Mariela." Ryan looked back at Mariela. "She needs a new dress for dinner tonight at the Mona Lisa."

"With you?" Mariela dropped her voice a bit. Her eyes took in Lisa's jeans and sneakers, then focused on the hair clip holding up a riot of curls.

Ryan shook his head. "Not really. A friend of the family, you could say."

Lisa seemed to pay their conversation no mind as she walked over to a rack with a beaded red dress and studied the lacy layers as they fell from the hanger.

"She's definitely not who you usually come in shopping for, Lucky Charm."

Ryan thought about making a joke but remembered his earlier resolve not to get into it. He decided on another non-descript shrug of his shoulders. "That one's history. They all come and go around here, anyway."

He'd been dating Erin Sjostrom, a tall Nordic beauty from the European poker circuit off-and-on for the last two years. She liked being seen with him, and Ryan never turned down the chance to be caught with eye candy—it took the pressure off him. When people got what they expected—poker player with hot blonde European girlfriend—they lived with their grand assumptions and rarely pressed him with questions.

Endorsements and magazine covers on the pro poker circuit didn't go to guys who preferred to stay home with their grandpa and dog.

When Erin took up with a professional golfer in a tournament around Christmas time, Ryan simply closed out the account he'd opened in her name here in the boutique. They were more of a mutually beneficial business transaction than a relationship, anyway.

But just like everyone else in Vegas, the only details Mariela knew about the poker circuit's so-called most eligible bachelor came strictly from what she saw on the surface.

And Ryan didn't see any reason to change the general school of thought. He wasn't going to be putting on the act much longer. He could live up to everyone else's expectations for a few more hours.

In his heart, he'd known it was time to make a change, and it felt right that the Shamrocks for Students tournament would be his last time behind a poker table. He didn't know what he'd be doing next, but he'd been holding 'em and folding 'em for almost a decade now.

He could feel that inner restlessness for the next challenge deep in his soul.

And being restless in Las Vegas rarely led to anything good.

The road to retirement would start in a few hours with easy few rounds of play in the company of some celebrities and high rollers who were giving money to the Shamrock Foundation, a fund that supported schools and students. The Foundation would collect the money from this tournament, culminating on St. Patrick's Day.

He knew there would be some silly photo ops with people who all wanted a piece of the phenom who'd won the last four Global Poker Challenge rings. Then Saturday morning, the real work would start when he sat down at the table and took the first look at the cards dealt to him.

And then, by Sunday, it would all be over.

And so would the only career he'd really ever known.

It took more than luck to win at a poker table. It took skill. And one of the greatest skills Ryan McBride had cultivated was to not give anything away unnecessarily.

"Lisa? Do you see anything you like?" Ryan stepped away from the counter.

"I'm honestly not sure where to begin. I haven't dressed up in a while. Being a high school drama teacher tends to keep you low-key. Lots of late nights and rehearsals." She wiggled the left half of a ratty pair of Chucks in his direction.

"I see that." The casual, canvas shoes branded her—loudly—as a tourist. "Well, Mariela can help you with whatever you need."

Lisa crooked her finger and wiggled it in the age-old sign for "come here." Ryan walked over to the rack closest to her. She looked at the red dress again, then picked up the heavy cardstock with the price tag and quickly dropped it from her fingers.

She leaned in and spoke in a whisper. "Is there any other place nearby? This stuff is all beautiful, but dresses with price tags that show numbers before a comma are just way out of my budget."

"Not any shops that you could get to and back in time for the dinner reservation."

He wanted to tell her it wasn't really his problem. He wanted to tell her he had to get ready for his work obligations tonight. He wanted to stick to his plan—drop her off and keep on moving.

But something about the look on Lisa's face stopped him.

Her eyes were wide, the same deep color as a sweet golden candy he used to take out of a jar next to Pops' recliner so many years ago. Her gaze darted around the room, unable to land on any one rack or dress with any kind of focus. As Ryan studied Lisa a little more closely, he noticed that her breathing was coming in a fashion that registered as a little shallower than a person's normal rate of inhalation and exhalation.

He'd seen it across the table more times than he could count.

The onset of panic. The moment when someone realized they were in over their head. In a poker match, he'd stare an opponent's fear down, and then ride it to a tall pile of colorful chips coming his way.

But he couldn't just stare Lisa down. Whatever this mess was, she was also the great-granddaughter of a long-lost friend of his grandfather's. And while he didn't really care what this woman or her great-grandmother were up to—as long as it all came to an end before anyone exchanged an "I do"—he did care what Pops thought. A lot.

And for his sake, Ryan would at least treat this woman the way his grandfather would expect.

He reached in his back pocket and pulled out his wallet, then turned toward the marble counter at the back.

"Mariela!"

The impeccably coiffured woman looked up as Ryan shattered the silence in the small boutique.

"Heads up." Ryan tossed his credit card through the air. It landed on the slick stone in front of Mariela with a small smack. "Anything she wants. You know the deal."

She nodded. "Indeed, I do. Glad to have you back in the store, Lucky Charm. I'll take care of her."

"Ryan, that's not necessary. Really." Lisa started to say more, but Ryan cut her off. It was just money. One dress from this boutique wasn't going to break him. It never had before. And there had been plenty.

Plenty of girls. Plenty of gifts. Plenty of swipes on that card.

Ryan McBride didn't *have* to do anything. Except when it came to the man who'd raised him and taught him everything he knew—about life and poker.

"Look, your great-grandmother is marrying my Pops. That makes us siblings or cousins or something. I'm an only child and I haven't seen my cousins since I was probably five years old. So, Merry Christmas or something, Cuz."

Ryan raised an eyebrow and gave Lisa a big grin, then checked his watch. He needed to get going. He needed to get ready for tonight. He had rituals he always went through before sitting down at a poker table.

But most of all, he needed to not get rivered—losing on the last card, in Texas Hold 'Em terms—by unchecked thoughts of a honey-haired pseudo-relative before he walked into the last big tournament he would ever play.

He decided to let that be the last word, to head back out to the grand, light-filled, ornate Italian renaissance-style hallway before Lisa could disagree or show gratitude. Either would have bothered him. He didn't want the gesture to take on any kind of life of its own.

It just was what it was. Another swipe on the limitless credit card.

LISA'S ROOM WASN'T ready yet, so after Mariela gave her the full Vegas shopping treatment, Lisa boarded the express elevator and found herself whisked up to the top of the Renaissance Grand. The elevator's swift motion made her stomach flutter just like it had with the sight of every price tag in the Rosé Boutique.

And every time she thought about Ryan McBride.

Thankfully, Lisa stood alone in the elevator—because she wasn't about to talk about that.

Not even with that annoying little voice in her head.

Actually...*absolutely not* with that annoying little voice in her head. It had a tendency to not shut up. And she'd never make it in Vegas with that voice telling her to check out Ryan McBride one more time.

As Lisa reached the door, Nana walked out with Bill, who'd come by to slowly escort her to dinner. They clearly wanted some alone time before sitting down to eat.

That suited Lisa just fine, as she wanted some alone time of her own.

She wanted to be alone with her thoughts, and a quick shower before dinner seemed the best way to do that.

But despite her resolve in the elevator, as Lisa washed the shampoo out of her hair, she realized she wasn't actually alone. Lisa had to admit she was outnumbered. By her own stupid, scattered brain. Everything ran around in her mind like hungry ants at a summer picnic. Even though she taught drama for a living, she knew she didn't need any more unscripted drama in her own life, for Pete's sake.

Lisa stared at her reflection in the bathroom mirror. Damp curls brushed her shoulders and her face glowed with the recent application of moisturizer. A dress that cost a month's worth of her salary hung on a hook just behind her.

It all felt surreal, this shiny, slick stone and bright lights experience. As she smoothed foundation on her face, then dusted blush across her cheekbones, she remembered her years in New York, trying to catch a break on Broadway.

Back then, she'd craved this—the spotlights, the elegant dresses, the ability to dress up and chameleon yourself into someone at the far rainbow end of your imagination.

But today it just all felt very fake, like discovering an heirloom ring held cut glass instead of a diamond.

She'd grown up in the years since she'd returned to Texas. She'd invested in the lives of her students, and seeing their confidence had begun to give her a lasting confidence of her own—not something manufactured for a performance on a stage.

Lisa dried her hair, then arranged it on her head in a twist, securing the base with a handful of bobby pins and spraying the curls on top with a liberal sheen of hairspray. As she played with the placement of the curls and the sharper edges of her thoughts, a knock sounded at the door.

She looked down with hesitation at the plush white terry cloth robe she was still wearing, then shrugged her shoulders. Likely it was just someone coming to offer turndown service. This was Las Vegas. Renaissance Grand staff members had probably caught guests in things far more risqué than the hotel-provided bathrobe.

A second round of rapping sounded at the door.

"Hold on! I'm coming!" Lisa shouted. The suite was so large it reminded her of her college apartment.

Well, the size did, anyway. She didn't see any particle board-based, some-assembly-required furniture or thrift store finds.

Lisa opened the door a crack.

It wasn't turndown service. If anything, what she saw in the sliver of space made her heart rate turn up a few clicks.

Ugh, there went that voice in her head again. Couldn't the fire alarm go off and drown this voice out?

The fire alarm is about to go off. Look in front of you. That's a solid three alarms, right there.

Black hair.

Black button-down shirt, open at the neck and crisp with a sheen of starch and precision under a tailored black sport coat.

Dark lightweight wool pants came to an end atop a pair of black leather shoes that reminded a documentary she'd watched the other day on the Riviera.

And a set of midnight blue eyes that reminded her of nothing she'd ever seen before in her life.

Alarm.

Alarm.

Alarm.

Lisa fought a battle on multiple fronts, trying to make the voice in her head *shut-the-craps-table-up*, as she simultaneously tried to speak through a throat gone dry the instant she realized he wasn't here to turn down the sheets.

She wasn't sure she'd turn down anything Ryan McBride suggested when he was looking like that.

"Pops panicked and called me, thinking you wouldn't know how to get to dinner. He wouldn't settle down until I promised I'd come get you."

She tugged the lapel of the bathrobe upwards. Her throat still felt like the sandy Nevada desert all around this town of lights.

"Can I come in?" His voice sounded flat, the exact opposite of the current flips and dives of Lisa's heart rate. Of course, *he* was in control. He lived here. He was used to seeing beautiful people all the time.

It wasn't her fault she lived on an island in Texas and only saw teenagers with acne problems all day.

Lisa didn't want to move. She didn't want to speak. Anything she could do right now was only going to embarrass herself somehow, she just knew it.

But...she couldn't just leave him out in the hallway.

Lisa stood behind the door as she again pulled it open, suddenly self-conscious of standing there in her bathrobe—in spite of her earlier nonchalance when she thought she'd just be encountering a member of the hotel staff.

Channel someone braver and prettier, Lisa. You can do this. Play the part.

"Sure, come on in." She tried to affect a nice, cool, Grace Kelly tone to her voice. Absently, she smoothed a stray wisp of hair behind her ear, once, twice, three times.

She could not let him know she gave a rodent's hindquarters about any of this.

He walked in swiftly, then stopped abruptly and looked out the window across the back of the suite. "Glad they took care of you and Gina Mae. That's a pretty great view. Mine's similar."

"You said you live here?" Lisa crossed her arms tightly, hugging her ribcage. Her gaze fell on Ryan's arms, hands pressed nonchalantly in his pockets, and a crazy thought scurried across her mind, like a squirrel darting for an acorn across a yard.

She remembered how toned his arms had looked earlier. And suddenly, she wondered what it would feel like to have them pressing around the white, fuzzy cover-up instead of her own slightly self-protective gesture.

"In the condo tower over there." He pointed at a building that sat off at a forty-five-degree angle from the main hotel, across an expanse of pools and clubhouses and fountains below. "That's mine up there on the top left corner."

With her eyes, Lisa followed the trail Ryan created with his finger. The windows were twice as tall as the rest of the floors and an oversized porch wrapped around the corner.

"Wow. I bet you do have a great view." Clearly, Ryan lived in the penthouse suite. She didn't even want to think about what that would cost. Probably more than her teacher's salary would generate for...oh, the next hundred years or so.

"I'm not there much."

Lisa detected a hint of something that sounded an awful lot like regret in his simple sentence. She'd been analyzing and coaching others in the art of tone and voice for a long time. The subtle pauses between syllables, or a catch of breath at just the right time, or a particular inflection always caught her ear's attention.

What she'd never quite mastered was the art of inquiry. She'd never be an investigator. She wanted to ask why; wanted to find out what he meant.

And then she heard another voice in her head.

One she never listened to, no matter what.

Her mother's voice.

Lisa never thought about her mother. Annelle Fleming never had much wisdom to spare for her young daughter. But she'd said one thing so many times that Lisa couldn't help but hear it in her mind, over every other sound in Las Vegas. Some memories were just that powerful, no matter how tightly you tried to keep them locked away.

Some secrets are just best kept, Lisa, the inner drawl locked inside her head said.

Lisa learned early not to ask questions of her mother. Not even so much as a *why* on the day Annelle left for good.

While Lisa fought it out with her internal deliberations, Ryan spoke again, cutting off her opportunity.

"It takes a few minutes to get down to the restaurant. How much longer do you need to get ready?"

In a way, the shift in conversation relieved Lisa. She shouldn't care what Ryan McBride thought or why he was never home. All she really had room to care about was making sure Nana was happy tonight and subsequently solving how she would get her great-grandmother out of this crazy engagement and back home without breaking her heart.

"About five minutes." She patted the bottom of her twist of curls. "All I need to do is get my dress."

Ryan turned away from the window. "So, you found something? Was Mariela helpful?"

"Oh yes. She had some great ideas."

The serious look on Ryan's face made Lisa tighten her arms once again around her torso. She could feel his stare fall on her like the closing of the curtain at the end of a play. The bathrobe had been made of thick, plush material, and yet, she felt as exposed as if she'd been wrapped in nothing but a cheap sheet with a bad thread count.

Lisa took a step backward, then another. "I'll just go finish dressing."

She turned away from his heavy gaze and headed back toward the expansive bathroom. The more distance between her and that stare, the better. She closed the tall wooden door and leaned back against it for a moment.

This morning, she'd gone to school to teach one last round of classes before Spring Break. She'd planned on coming home and working in the backyard, getting her landscape beds ready for a season of blooms and fragrance. She'd longed for a week of tranquility, a change from the hectic pace of being around high school drama and drama students all day.

Instead, she'd been greeted with the news of her great-grandmother's Internet-enabled engagement and a pair of plane tickets. A few hours later, she found herself in the newest, fanciest hotel in Las Vegas, surrounded by non-stop lights and glitter, about to slip on the most expensive dress she'd ever owned, paid for by a man she'd just met.

It all seemed like something out of a movie.

Only this time, she wasn't acting.

There was no script telling her what to say. No stage directions telling her what to do.

Lisa Fleming was on her own.

And she couldn't tell if Ryan McBride—with his cool James Dean air and eyes that looked at her as though he'd knew what she was thinking—was a villain or a hero in this scene she'd been inadvertently cast in.

Lisa walked to the hook on the closet door and raised the bag containing her dress. She took a step back and looked at it with a slightly skeptical eye. It was so different than anything she'd ever worn before.

But Mariela insisted she'd needed the dress. Lisa had tried to explain that it was too short, too sheer, too frivolous for her. The playful wisp of a skirt, made entirely of a riot of foot-long black ostrich-style feathers, reminded her of a sassy little number she'd seen in a recent celebrity gossip magazine.

"*This is Las Vegas. Everyone's playing a part. No one wants to be themselves*, Cara Mia," Mariela explained in heavily accented English, silencing Lisa's requests for something more simple, more tailored.

Lisa knew all about playing a part. She'd spent her entire adult life on one stage or another.

What she didn't know, as she slid the dress over her head and tugged her arms through the lacy cap sleeves, was how this story would end.

Lisa slid her feet into a pair of towering satin heels and threaded a pair of long, chunky gold earrings in her ears. Then she closed her eyes, took a deep breath, and tried to imagine the lights on the stage.

Tonight was no different than any other time she'd stepped in front of an audience.

She was playing a role.

Lisa Fleming, Las Vegas bridesmaid. Audience of one—Gina Mae Fleming. It didn't matter how unsure she was of this dress. It didn't matter how she didn't want to be indebted to Ryan McBride for paying for it with one practiced flick of a black plastic rectangle. It didn't matter that she had no idea how she was going to get Nana out of here without saying "I do."

All that mattered was that Nana enjoyed tonight and enjoyed her time with her old friend, even though it could go no further than a few days of reunion.

Lisa took another deep breath and forced it up into the corners of her mouth. Shoulders back, eyes ahead. Hand on the door, she smiled brightly.

It was time for the performance of her life.

Chapter Three

AFTER BEING IN VEGAS for so many years, Ryan McBride looked out at the skyline in front of him and feared he'd become immune to the extraordinary. There was always a brighter light, a bigger jackpot, a more beautiful woman.

He heard the gentle crack of the bathroom door and the tell-tale tap of high heels on marble behind him. He turned around and instantly, as a lightning-quick shock pulsed through him, Ryan knew his theory had been incorrect.

He could still feel.

Raw. Primitive. Instinctive. He hadn't planned for this quick-trigger physical reaction to the woman walking toward him, and he couldn't control it.

He'd heard of the little black dress. Mariela had helped Lisa pick out one heck of one, emphasis on *little*.

As in little lacy fabric. Little flyaway feather skirt with lots of leg. And very little left to the imagination.

She strode toward him confidently, with a megawatt smile on her face, looking like a model pacing a catwalk. He couldn't believe this was the same Lisa from earlier. This woman wasn't trailing in anyone's wake or nervously flipping price tags.

This woman was confident, put-together, and downright sexy.

She flipped her hands out at her sides, palms up. "Will this work for the Mona Lisa?"

It would work for anywhere in Vegas. But Ryan hesitated in saying that, even though he didn't quite know why.

"I guess that's a yes." She stood there, hand perched on her right hip. Ryan studied the curve of her body, framed by the angle of her bent arm. He wanted to slide his arm in there and wrap it around the small of her back, draw her close, and find out what other surprises she'd been hiding beneath that casual travel outfit and the expression of skepticism she'd worn all day.

"It is." Ryan nodded, hoping he hadn't totally given away his approval.

He wasn't used to giving away his hand. And he still didn't know anything about Lisa Fleming or her great-grandmother. Or how he was going to keep Pops from making this huge marriage mistake he'd surprised Ryan with earlier today.

"You ready to head down?" Ryan kept his hands firmly in his pockets so he didn't make the wrong move and reach out for Lisa's hand.

Or that inviting curve that flared just around her hip.

Pops had called this his engagement dinner and set all this in motion, but the key word for Ryan tonight was *disengagement*. Both in a matrimonial sense for Pops, and a mental one for himself.

Lisa didn't say much as they wound through the hallways of the Renaissance Grand. Her head turned back and forth, as though she didn't want to miss a thing.

"First time in Vegas?" Ryan fished for chit-chat as he pushed the button to the elevator which would take them directly to the Mona Lisa, at the top of one of the Renaissance Grand's towers.

She turned her head away from a painting and back toward Ryan. "Believe it or not, yes."

He held the elevator door back and gestured for Lisa to go first. "A Vegas virgin. Well, I hope you enjoy your trip."

She looked at him, then dropped her gaze away. The curls on the top of her fancy twist hairstyle swayed slightly with the sudden movement. "Well, I will if I..."

"If you what?"

The elevator doors slid open to a lacquered world of gold and white and red and black. The color theme matched a deck of cards.

And Ryan wanted desperately to call Lisa's bluff. To find out what she was hiding behind that open-ended sentence. But his hesitation cost him the moment.

"Mr. McBride," an older gentleman with an Italian accent held open the door in front of them. "Welcome back to the Mona Lisa. Your guests have already arrived. Right this way, please."

He gestured with his arm, ushering them into a world of metallic shine and good, old-fashioned Las Vegas high rolling. The Mona Lisa was reserved for the highest level of visitors to the Renaissance Grand. Celebrities, royalty, and those who weren't afraid to pile up chips at the tables in the gaming area below.

Thanks to winning four Global Poker Challenge rings, Ryan now fell into the first category and the last. And in Las Vegas, Nevada, those two and a GPC ring were enough to get one treated like royalty. There weren't many doors in this town that closed to Ryan McBride these days.

Except for wedding chapel doors.

But that was by his own design, and he planned to keep it that way. For both himself and Pops.

"Hey, there they are!" Pops almost bounced out of his seat the moment his eyes caught sight of his grandson. He waved an arm with high enthusiasm.

Ryan felt like everyone in the quiet restaurant had paused and taken note of them, thanks to his grandfather's boisterous greeting. He'd always thought of himself as a "keep your head down" kind of guy, but it was hard to be mad when Pops was clearly acting from an enthusiasm more commonly seen in teenage love, not rekindled romances between people nearing the century mark in age.

Pops wasn't the only one who was turning heads in the candlelit room. Ryan didn't know what he was having a harder time believing. That Pops had turned back time and become an adolescent again, or that the quiet, unsure schoolteacher had the attention of every man in one of the most exclusive restaurants in Las Vegas.

Lisa Fleming had certainly captured his attention. He could usually shake distractions. Being able to do so was critical in his profession.

He couldn't keep from tracing Lisa's curves, from the way her stiletto heels made her calf muscles more clearly defined, to the upper thighs just barely peeking out through the feathered skirt, to her most womanly curves up a little bit higher. The realization that in the last ten minutes, he'd just checked out Pops's step-great-granddaughter-to-be more times than he'd cared to admit confirmed the one thing he'd been forced to admit to himself lately.

Ryan McBride was losing his edge.

His passion for the game and the single-minded focus he needed to be great, to win, was slipping.

But apparently not his passion for a good-looking woman.

And that scared him even more than the thought of cashing in his chips and moving on to whatever would come next in his career and life.

Pops had already pulled out Lisa's chair by the time they got to the table. "My dear, you look gorgeous."

He kissed her gently on one cheek.

Ryan looked away, trying to keep his thoughts from shifting away from the curves he'd been noticing earlier and over to the curve of her lower lip—and what it would be like to give her a kiss of his own.

Something about her unexpected transformation tonight was throwing every part of him into overdrive. And it needed to stop. He had about ninety minutes over dinner to start laying the framework to get Pops to come to his senses. With the celebrity round later tonight and the full charity poker tournament taking up most of his next two days, he wouldn't have much free time before the wedding date to execute his plan to stop the wedding from happening.

And as the *maître d'* dropped the cloth napkin gently into Ryan's lap, signaling the beginning of his dinner time, Ryan knew he only had a matter of minutes to come up with a plan.

"I hope we didn't keep you waiting too long," Lisa said. She leaned forward and Ryan was once again distracted by some of her more prominent curves as they brushed the edge of the table.

He groaned a little bit in self-reproach, then looked the other way.

"No, they've taken good care of us here." Pops patted Gina Mae on the hand. "Is something wrong, Ryan?"

Of all the times for Pops's hearing aid to actually work. "No, sir. Nothing at all."

Well, nothing except needing a plan, a new job, and to stop thinking about how downright hot the woman next to him looked.

Especially to stop thinking about how downright hot Lisa Fleming looked.

His edge wasn't as sharp as it used to be, and he knew it. But he still knew he could spot a gold digger. And the way Lisa Fleming transformed herself from shrinking violet into full-bloomed crimson rose in just a matter of hours told Ryan his instinct was more than likely right on this one. She turned from caterpillar to butterfly with a seamless ease that showed she wasn't new to this sort of dressing up.

"Great," Pops said. "I ordered us some *hors d'oeuvres*. And a bottle of champagne. You can't celebrate an engagement without a little celebratory drink, right, Gina Mae?"

The apples of her cheeks rounded and were brushed with the soft glow of candlelight as she smiled. "No. And this is definitely a celebration. Who would have guessed we'd be here after all these years?"

"Do you know how Las Vegas became the wedding capital of the world?" Pops leaned slightly toward Lisa.

She shook her head, and the angles and facets of her large golden earrings picked up the candlelight and reflected twinkles back. "No, I actually don't. I don't know much about Las Vegas at all."

Pops leaned back, adopting the classic raconteur's pose, and tapped his fingertips together in a triangle shape. Ryan recognized the signature move well. If he'd been at a table, he'd have gone all in. Pops was just that easy to read.

"In 1912, the state of California passed a three-day waiting period for issuing marriage licenses. They said it was to protect people who'd been drinking too much from making bad decisions. Anyway, Nevada decided they had no such issues, and responded with some marketing of their own. They said Nevada was the easiest place to make the best—or worst—decision of your life. Let the chips fall where they may, right, Ryan?"

"Of course, Pops." Ryan actually hadn't heard that story before, but he was too busy trying to turn empty thoughts into a plan to become California—in a manner of speaking—and stop the couple across from him from making a bad decision.

"You know, ladies, my grandson here is pretty good with the chips." He nodded his head in affirmation of Ryan's skills. "Son, you should take Lisa on a tour of the casino after dinner since she said she doesn't know much about Vegas."

Ryan flipped open his menu. "I've got to work tonight, Pops. I know you've got wedding brain, but the Shamrocks for Students tournament is all weekend long. It's my last one, so I've got to be there from start to finish. Remember, we talked about this earlier in the week? Besides, I'm sure Lisa and Gina Mae are tired from their travel today."

He didn't want to be rude to Pops' guests—even if they were proven to be the gold diggers he took them for, Pops hadn't raised Ryan to be disrespectful. But he also hadn't been raised to be a babysitter. Ryan had been raised to make hay while the sun was shining and to be the embodiment of a thousand other similar proverbs Pops quoted over and over through the years.

And tonight, he had to work. He had to give it his all one final time.

"Well, I'd forgotten about that. But, Ryan, this is Las Vegas. No one comes here to sleep." Pops laughed as he spoke.

"I'm sure I can find something to do, Bill. That's ok. No one needs to be my babysitter."

Had Lisa read his mind? Ryan thought it was funny she'd used the same description he'd been thinking.

The waiter walked over to them with a chilled bottle of champagne and held it out before the guests of honor.

"Well, I don't want you to be lonely. This is a weekend for celebration." He tapped the cream-colored label affixed to the front of the cool green glass bottle. "And this is the perfect way to start."

As the golden liquid poured into the flute in front of him, Pops lifted the glass. White bubbles foamed at the opening, like miniature fireworks in a fluffy sky. "To our new family. And new beginnings. May we all be grateful for the chances we're given and the love in our lives."

Bill turned his head away from the younger generation and looked straight at the woman he planned to marry. Gina Mae effortlessly raised her glass and clinked her stem with his in the age-old salute of toasting.

Ryan was surprised to not hear any affirmations of Pops's words from Lisa. She sat straight as the neck of the champagne bottle next to her, shoulders back. She raised her glass slightly, but although her eyes were focused on the lovebirds nearby, Ryan could clearly see she was looking through them, not at them.

He took in her whole face carefully, as studiously as he'd cataloged all her curves as they'd walked to the table earlier. The lower lip he'd traced with his own thoughts was now pressed deliberately and tightly against her narrower top lip. She'd curved the corners up enough that anyone who gave her a casual glance would think she was smiling.

But Ryan knew better.

She was hiding something.

The fire in his belly that had been missing for a while came back with the kick of a white-hot ember. Ryan wanted to know what she was thinking. And once he figured it out, he wouldn't be afraid to use it to his advantage in this current matrimonial situation.

"What?" Lisa placed her glass on the table in front of her and looked at Ryan. "Is something wrong?"

Ryan raised his glass. "Not at all."

She didn't look convinced. But, he figured, that was okay. He wasn't particularly convinced everything was going to plan for her, either.

The waiter came back and brought several plates of appetizers, placing them in front of Ryan.

"This is courtesy of the Renaissance Grand, Mr. McBride. It's a pleasure to have you dining with us tonight," the *maître d'* stood just off to the side of the table.

"It's always a pleasure to be here, Jerome," Ryan replied politely. Everyone at the Renaissance Grand knew him and took care of his every need—even ones he didn't know he had. Once he announced he was leaving the tour, would they still place large, round croutons topped with a tomato and kalamata olive mix in front of him? Or were his days of bruschetta, drinks on the house, and a concierge who took care of last-minute ideas and whims soon to be a thing of the past?

If that's what happened, he'd just have to deal with it. Besides, he didn't know if he'd even stay in Las Vegas. After years of calculating an opponent's next move, next card, Ryan didn't know his own next step.

He'd made the decision to move on, but unfortunately, it was not soothing the sense of restlessness that had been hanging around his soul for almost a year now.

The small party moved through several courses quickly. Ryan let Pops do most of the talking. If he was honest, he just didn't know what to say to Gina Mae or Lisa, knowing that all he truly wanted was for them to get on a plane and go home before they'd brought any permanent change to Pops's life. And his own.

Pops smiled, looking like a high schooler on his way to his first prom. Ryan hadn't seen his grandfather look so at ease in years. Ever since he'd moved out to Las Vegas, there had been a sadness around him that Ryan couldn't place.

In the last few hours, though, Ryan could see the grandfather he used to know. The one who cracked jokes, who loved a good adventure, who always had a helping hand and a listening ear. Ryan had almost forgotten that side of Pops.

But he couldn't help but feel like it was back for all the wrong reasons. And he just wasn't going to be an enabler. It stood out to him that Pops had forgotten the whole conversation they'd had on Monday about the Shamrocks for Students tournament.

Ryan hadn't wanted to admit that age was catching up to Pops, but forgetting the tournament, keeping secrets about bringing Gina Mae to Vegas and these crazy wedding plans—something just didn't make sense right now.

Actually—nothing made sense right now.

This whole spur-of-the-moment Vegas wedding scenario didn't make sense.

And neither did the fact that Ryan couldn't keep himself from catching glances at Lisa Fleming out of the corner of his eye.

"Lisa, I'm sorry my grandson seems to be working tonight. You can come help your Nana and me pick out flowers for the wedding."

"No, that's okay. I don't want to intrude. I'm sure there are plenty of things for me to do in Las Vegas." Lisa shook her head, then turned toward Ryan with a practiced smile. "Not everything around here has to lead to trouble, right?"

The only trouble he could see was looking right at him. Once he got this lady in the black lace dress and her great-grandmother back on a plane to Texas, Las Vegas would have a whole lot less trouble in town.

Chapter Four

LISA KNEW RYAN DIDN'T want her here. She also knew she was bored, even in one of the fastest-paced cities in America. But she hadn't come here to vacation, to see shows, to gamble, or to eat at one of the legendary Las Vegas buffets.

Maybe if she just slipped here in the back of this tournament room, Ryan wouldn't know and she could alleviate some of her boredom.

Lisa took one of the few remaining seats in the Venezia Ballroom. It wasn't quite the back row like she'd hoped, but it was near the edge of the room and seemed like it would suit her purpose—whatever that actually was. She didn't know anything for certain right now.

A young blonde, her hair falling over her shoulders in glossy, perfectly sprayed waves, lowered herself into the aisle seat next to Lisa.

"I'm actually going to need that seat in a few minutes," she said. "I'm with NCN, the National Card Network. I've got a live interview with Lucky Charm at the break."

"Oh, you mean Ryan McBride?" It seemed so strange to Lisa how many people referred to a grown man by such a silly nickname.

"Yes. He told me he has an announcement to make."

Surely he wasn't going to talk about his grandfather's upcoming wedding. That seemed a silly thing to announce on a TV network. Actually, the idea of a TV network covering card games seemed pretty silly, too.

Except...there had been a time when she'd have considered it a huge step in her career to have been given a job like this girl had. There had been a time, not so terribly long ago, when Lisa would have taken any job in film, on TV, or on stage if it had meant keeping her dream of being an actress alive.

"Did he say what it was?" Lisa whispered back. She really had no business asking, but the curiosity was definitely getting the better of her. She'd never met a man like Ryan McBride. He threw around an AmEx Black like it was a children's toy. He was treated with almost royal deference by everyone in this microcosmic little alternate reality known as the Renaissance Grand. But for all that he acted like a cool enigma, he *was* devoted to his Pops, she would certainly give him that.

The blonde uncrossed, then recrossed her legs under her short charcoal-sequined skirt and scooted forward to perch on the edge of her chair. "No," she said with a short clip off the edge of the single syllable. "But he never says much."

"Tell me about it." Lisa also moved to the edge of her seat and leaned slightly left, in order to get a better look at Ryan.

To his right sat Kramer Forde, a Hollywood veteran whose gray hair had moved him from the action hero roles he got thirty years ago to more distinguished casting, but hadn't diminished his leading man popularity. To his left was social media entrepreneur Caleb Walsh, who'd just taken his mobile messaging interface company public and made a fortune that neared a billion dollars in just a matter of hours after the stock market's opening bell. Across from Ryan was a man Lisa didn't recognize. He wore a red hoodie and a white baseball cap, each with a logo embroidered on them.

"Who's that?" Lisa leaned back just enough to catch the blonde reporter's attention.

"Breck Goulding. Do you not watch much poker?" She kept her eyes glued straight ahead.

"Um, no. This is a first for me."

Kramer Forde pushed an impressively tall pile of chips to the middle of the green felt-covered table, then slumped in his chair and ran his hands over his face in frustration as Ryan flipped his cards over with a practiced flick.

"Well, that's that." The reporter looked at Lisa, then stood up. "So how did you wind up coming to watch by yourself?"

"Lisa?" Ryan pushed through the door in the barrier separating the game from the spectators.

So much for remaining off his radar. She felt a small trickle of sweat trickle down the crease between her shoulder blades and tried to tell herself it was from the hot stage lights overhead, not nerves.

Lisa looked at the reporter, who now looked between her and a dark-eyed Ryan with a double-take that could easily be read by even a poker novice. The little blonde was not keeping her confusion a secret.

"I...well...I know him." Lisa nodded in Ryan's direction, though she didn't need to. The fact that he was quickly closing the distance between them said more than her spur-of-the-moment awkward attempt at an explanation.

All of a sudden, the reporter's eyes narrowed to slits. Lisa read that expression clearly as well. Maybe Lisa had more skill at calling people's bluff than she'd previously thought, because the reporter's look was pure jealousy. No doubt about it.

"Hey, Lucky Charm, you ready?" The reporter reached out for Ryan's arm and ran her fingers slowly from his shoulder to elbow.

Lisa felt a little jealousy of her own creep up, but she couldn't place why. She was only here because she needed to kill some time while her grandmother dreamed up wedding details with Bill. She was only here watching a celebrity poker tournament because an hour ago, it seemed preferable to pretending to be involved in the wedding plans. That felt like lying; like she was giving her support to what was going on.

But all of a sudden, this felt just as awkward. Because even though Lisa tried to push the thought out of her mind as soon as it popped in there, she found herself wondering what it would be like to be as casual with Ryan McBride as the blonde with the perfectly styled beachy waves seemed to be.

Ryan tugged his arm back, but the reporter's hot pink nails threaded between his fingers and tugged. She didn't quite have him where she wanted him, but she was certainly trying.

"Yeah." He disengaged and ran a hand through his hair. "Where do you want me?"

She smiled, the expression as polished and hard as a diamond. "You name it, Lucky Charm. I'll set up wherever you want."

Lisa couldn't contain a most unladylike snort.

The look she got in return could have frozen the entire Nevada desert.

"I'm going to need you to stand somewhere else, Miss." Disdain coated the blonde's words like burned icing atop a sugar cookie.

Ryan freed his hand from the young woman's grasp and reached out, grabbing Lisa by the wrist. "No you don't, Emma. She's with me."

As instinctively as the little snorty laugh had come earlier, now her best Broadway smile flew up to Lisa's lips.

So...Ryan needed a buffer from Little Miss National Card Network. Well, Lisa didn't know anything about poker, and she didn't know anything about Vegas but the stereotypes.

But if there was one thing Lisa Fleming did know, it was acting. She knew history, theory, and method.

And she knew she could help Ryan McBride out right now.

She owed him. He hadn't cared when she'd said she couldn't afford a dress in that boutique. He'd just bought her this red carpet-worthy dress without so much as a second thought so she could be appropriately dressed for her grandmother's rehearsal dinner. He'd even thrown down that credit card again and paid for the meal, at what Lisa knew had to be a significant cost.

Even though she wanted Nana to come home at the end of this trip without making any life-altering changes, she did recognize that Nana seemed happier than she'd been in so, so long. Her eyes had glowed with pride when she saw Lisa walk in wearing this fancy dress and her eyes had glowed when Bill McBride had toasted her as his first and last love.

And Lisa knew Ryan McBride's generosity—however cloaked behind a face Lisa could not read—had made both of those moments possible.

"Sorry it took me so long to get here," Lisa said, putting an extra dose of sugar in her voice in order to better sell the moment to Emma the reporter. "I had to get Nana settled with the spa menu so she could pick out all the wedding-day pampering."

Emma's jaw dropped. She touched her ear and paused, then nodded and signaled the cameraman with a raised, pink shellac-topped finger. "Thanks, Ricky. I'm here with the leader in tonight's celebrity round of the Shamrocks for Students tournament, the one and only Lucky Charm, Ryan McBride. Thanks for joining me, Lucky Charm. You said you had an important announcement to make tonight to National Card Network viewers. I figured it was going to be something to do with your career—I thought you'd be telling us you'd decided to go for a record-setting fifth consecutive world championship ring this season."

She put her hand on Lisa's shoulder and roughly pushed her into the shot. Lisa tried to keep the smile on her face, not quite knowing what the scorned little reporter was trying to do.

"But I had no idea you were going to announce to NCN viewers that poker's most eligible bachelor is off the market."

Ryan looked at Lisa and then at Emma. He opened his mouth to speak, but Emma let out a girlish squeal.

"The Lucky Charm is getting married! Congratulations!"

It took all the skill Lisa had as an actress to keep her jaw where it was supposed to be. *Just keep playing the part*, she reminded herself.

Only, she had no idea what part she was now playing. Surely Ryan would correct the misunderstanding.

He slipped an arm around Lisa's waist and pulled her tight against him. Lisa could feel the hard striations of muscles of chest and abs through the starched cotton of his button-down shirt.

"This is my fiancée, Lisa Fleming." Ryan gave Lisa's waist a squeeze and the camera a quick flash of a grin, framed by a short dusting of yesterday's five o'clock shadow.

"You heard it here first, card fans. So, Lucky Charm, how did you two meet?" Emma's smile dripped insincerity like an artificial sweetener.

The fans at home probably couldn't see the clench at the back of Emma's jawline, but Lisa could—all too clearly. She felt like putting a hand over her eyes to keep the young blonde from clawing them out.

Ryan's expression never wavered. "Well, it probably sounds old-fashioned, but we were introduced by our families. I knew the minute I met her, my life was going to change."

Emma's eyebrows raised skeptically. "Oh, really? What about you, Lisa? Did you know he was the one?"

Lisa thought quickly back to their first words in the airport, when she'd told him to get his luggage and move on. Life-changing, indeed. "To be honest, Emma, the whole thing has taken me by surprise."

Shock might be a better word.

At least when she passed out from the shock, Ryan's solid chest would be there to break her fall.

"Well, thanks for sharing your big news with us, Lucky Charm. Honestly, I didn't know what your big surprise was going to be." She tucked some blonde waves behind her ear in a self-protective manner. "You're leading tonight's chip count comfortably, so all in all a good night, right?"

Ryan kept his hand circled around Lisa's waist. She forced herself to remember she was just playing an unintentional role. It kept her from thinking about how long it had been since a good-looking man had pulled her close, wordlessly announcing to the world that she was his.

"Yes, Lisa's definitely *my* lucky charm." He looked up at the larger-than-life LCD screen above them, broadcasting this interview live to the spectators in the room. "There's one more thing, too, Emma."

Her brittle smile stayed virtually immobile. "Oh? What's that?"

"Shamrocks for Students will be my last tournament. I'm retiring from the Global Poker Challenge tour."

Lisa scanned the faces in the room as they processed Ryan's bombshell announcement. A man in a flame patterned shirt in the middle of the room shot visual daggers straight at her. Several others looked at her with expressions ranging from disdain to outright hostility. Lisa imagined this must have been how Yoko Ono felt when confronted by the Beatles faithful.

She wanted to tell them it wasn't her fault, that she had only known Ryan McBride for half a day. She wasn't his lucky charm, and she wasn't his fiancée.

But she couldn't break character.

And apparently, neither could Ryan, because before Emma even had a chance to provide commentary, he lifted his hand from Lisa's waist and pressed it against her hair, leaning her head toward him.

In front of one very hostile gallery of poker fans, he pressed his lips to Lisa's cheek.

A hoot came from the back corner of the audience. Then one decidedly strong wolf whistle.

Ryan adjusted the position of his hands and turned Lisa toward him. They were so close she could hear the shortness of his breath and smell the faint sandalwood and spice of his cologne. He threw a quick grin at the gathered crowd, then leaned in and locked his lips on Lisa's.

Lisa had been kissed hundreds of times when a role required it. Having chemistry with a co-star was an essential part of acting.

But she couldn't tell what Ryan McBride was playing at. He held her tightly and his lips pressed with some unspoken demand. Lisa heard the blood rushing in her ears as her own mouth met Ryan's lips and matched their strong, questing slide against hers. The rasp of the short hairs on his chin slid roughly against her skin, forcing her awareness of what was happening.

She'd kissed a lot of men that she barely knew in the name of theatre. But that was always about staying on script.

Ryan pulled away and a few more claps and whistles filled the room.

Emma the reporter stood, unmoving, and perhaps the only one more stunned than Lisa. "Well, there you have it, poker fans. The legendary Lucky Charm is cashing in his chips after this weekend's tournament. The tour won't be the same without you, Ryan McBride."

Lisa could hear the unspoken "And neither will I." Clearly, Emma had more than a small crush on Ryan and she didn't appreciate that it wasn't going to be reciprocated.

For her part, Lisa wanted to just keep smiling and keep going on with the show, like she'd done for so many meaningless kisses in meaningless roles. But Ryan still stood closer than a whisper to her. His arm slid back tightly around her waist. There was no way she could just move on to the next scene. Not until she figured out what was going on.

An assistant tapped Ryan on the shoulder. "Hey, the break's over. Time to get back."

"Okay." Ryan dropped his hand from Lisa's waist. The interview was over. So was the moment. Lisa shuffled to the side to let Ryan pass back through the door to the main gaming area.

A low buzz filled the room, the sound of the assembled crowd discussing Ryan's two bombshells. Distracted by the chatter and the celebrities coming back to the table under the lights, no one seemed to notice that Ryan McBride didn't say another word or give a glance back to the so-called lucky charm of his own life.

But Lisa did.

And as soon as all the eyes were focused back on the dealer and the rapid-fire flick of the cards, Lisa quietly slipped out of the room, unable to think about anything other than that kiss—and unable to understand why it felt like more than a role she was playing.

"MR. MCBRIDE?" CARLOS, a hotel staffer with a slight Caribbean accent called out across the breezeway.

Ryan stopped and turned around.

"Your fiancée is out by the pool."

"My what?"

"Your fiancée," Carlos repeated. "The one you introduced tonight in that interview with Emma Brown. The tour's going to miss you, Lucky Charm. I don't think anyone saw that coming."

They'd probably all be shocked to know Ryan hadn't seen it coming either. Sure, he knew he was retiring from the tour, but he had no idea why he'd introduced Lisa as his fiancée.

Or why he'd kissed her.

Or why he'd kissed her again. On the lips.

Or why—if he was honest with himself—he'd liked it.

In fact, if he knew the answers to those questions, he could probably use them as an explanation for his biggest loss in two years. He hadn't lasted long after he got back to the table. It served as more confirmation that he'd made the right decision to retire. He'd lost his edge. Kissing women he didn't know and folding early at a card table were two things he never did.

"Rod set her up in a cabana. Number thirty-six, I believe, sir." Carlos gestured toward the far end of the pool. "He said he knew you'd want us to take good care of her, since it looked like she was upset. We tried to help."

"Thanks, Carlos. I appreciate it." Ryan turned away from the path leading to his condo. He didn't know what Lisa Fleming had to be upset about. She'd scored an expensive dress, a Michelin-starred, multi-course dinner, and a kiss from the man named last year's Most Eligible Bachelor in Las Vegas.

Maybe the wedding between Pops and her nana had been called off and she was mourning the loss of the McBride gravy train. Typical gold digger behavior.

Ryan was about halfway to the striped cabana near the corner of the pool when he stopped himself. What was he doing? He'd already bought her dinner and that dress, and he'd only known her a handful of hours.

Of course, in Vegas time, that was like an eternity.

He stood there, unable to turn back toward his penthouse, but unwilling to get any closer to cabana thirty-six. Ryan shoved his hands in his pockets and stared at the still-heavy crowd milling about the poolside nightlife.

"Excuse me," a voice said, sounding just above a whisper.

Ryan stepped closer to the edge of the sidewalk and looked at the woman trying to walk by. She looked down at her shoes, causing her face to be veiled by the night shadows, but there was no mistaking that short feathered skirt.

"Lisa?"

She rolled her eyes up slightly. "Oh," she paused. The syllable came out as flat as a poker chip. "It's you."

There weren't a lot of people in Las Vegas who spoke to Ryan McBride that bluntly. "What do you mean by that?"

"You tell me what you mean by kissing me in front of a live studio audience, and then you'll get your answer." She stood up straight and pressed her shoulders back. The realignment of her posture made all her lace-covered curves fall into their proper place.

Although it was a balmy mid-March night, Ryan felt certain she was only a few degrees away from making steam come out her ears. The flush on Lisa's cheeks reminded him of a hot Nevada summer.

If he was perfectly honest with himself, when paired with that lacy little number she had on, everything about her was flaming hot. His own pulse flared a few notches as he stared her down.

"You tell me what you meant by not kissing back."

"What?"

Ryan almost couldn't believe he'd said that to her. But it had been a long time since he'd sat through such an ugly defeat at a poker table, and it seemed he was itching for some kind of confrontation to get the sting out of his system.

"You heard me. I thought you said you were a theatre teacher. Don't you know about acting?"

"Who are you, Lee Strasberg?" Her tawny eyes locked on him as they took on a flaming ember that turned them to the color of a good sherry. "And a similar question could be asked of you. Don't you know anything about gambling?"

He held up his right hand and let the moonlight wink off the diamonds crusting the edges of his latest Global Poker Challenge championship ring. "I know plenty about gambling, Doll."

"Well then, let me put it in terms you'll understand. You rolled the dice. And you lost. I don't want to kiss you, you cocky jerk. I want to get my Nana on a plane and get her out of this city before she makes the biggest mistake of her life." The fire sizzled in her eyes again. "And I'm not your doll, your lucky charm, or your fiancée."

He'd been enjoying getting the excess adrenaline from tonight's game out of his system so much that he almost retorted back without truly listening to what Lisa had said. He caught himself hard, like the jerk at the end of a bungee jump when the cord engages to stop the free fall.

"What did you say?"

Lisa spoke slowly, drawing out each syllable for emphasis. "I'm. Not. Your. Fiancée. Pretend or otherwise."

"I know that. The first part—what did you say first?"

"I want to go home." She broke into a song. He heard her mutter something about being home with armadillos in Amarillo...or something like that. He'd never heard the tune before.

Her voice was clear and self-assured. And although he had no idea why she was singing about an armadillo, he'd heard enough singers here in Las Vegas—megastars and lounge acts alike—to know that Lisa Fleming's voice was special, classically-trained and true.

"You live with armadillos?"

"No. It's a song called London Homesick Blues. It's about a guy who misses Texas. I know how he feels. I don't want to be here."

Ryan felt all the tension and frustration in his body let down. First, his shoulders relaxed, then a wave took over his body, down to his toes. The only thing that didn't let down was a keen awareness of Lisa Fleming's fiery eyes and black lace-wrapped body.

"So why are you here?"

She took a deep breath. "Because I'm trying to save Nana from herself. I'm a teacher—you know that. Anyway, today was the last day before Spring Break. I live with Nana, taking care of her, and when I walked through the door of the house today, Nana informed me that we were going on a Spring Break trip to Vegas. As I pressed her on why, she tells me this story of meeting her long-lost love again on Facebook. All I wanted to do this week was work in my garden. But I think something's wrong with Nana. This is so out of character for her. And if I don't stop her..."

Lisa's voice trailed off. She looked up at the stars shining in the clear Nevada night. A faint sparkle glinted in the corner of her eye. She blinked several times in rapid succession and the tear flicked away.

"So you didn't know about this?" Ryan couldn't believe that she might have been caught by surprise, just like he'd been when driving to the airport with Pops.

She shook her head. "Not a bit. I didn't even know she knew the password for the laptop. She can barely figure out the remote to work the TV. You said earlier you'd just found out today too, right?"

"Yeah. I had no idea. I bought Pops a new computer last year. He told me he was playing solitaire on it. Clearly, he's moved on to something a little less solitary."

They stood in silence for a moment. Ryan tried to process what Lisa had said. "I assumed you had to know. I figured you and your grandmother were both in it together."

Lisa pivoted on the toe of one high-heeled shoe. "You thought I was some kind of Vegas gold digger?"

He felt pretty confident that he could dispel the indignation in her voice by saying no. He could cloak it in the bland, plastic face he used when he was closing in on a pile of chips. The best poker sharks in the world rarely figured out what he was hiding. He felt pretty confident about being able to conceal his real thoughts from the theatre teacher.

But he didn't want to lie to her.

He didn't exactly know why, except that there'd been enough suspicion and mixed signals between them for one day.

Now that he realized they were on the same side, he began to wonder if maybe they could work as a team to achieve their goals.

Then she could go home to the armadillos, and he could go home to whatever he was going to do after he'd cashed in his last chip.

"Yeah, I pretty much did. Why else would Pops be planning something like this without telling me? And why would his bride-to-be bring along a granddaughter, except to try and pick up the single grandson. The truth is, I've made a lot of money out here in Las Vegas. You wouldn't be the first woman who's tried to trap me."

"Well, trust me, I'm not." She looked around nervously. "I don't even like thinking about it, but I'm worried about Nana. This isn't like her. It's like she has..."

"Alzheimer's or something?" Ryan completed her sentence as though it were his own.

"Yes. Exactly. How did you know?" The breathless relief in her voice drove Ryan's pulse up a few notches. He couldn't believe how fast his mind started down a different track now that the money-grubbing path had officially been shut down. It was like all bets were off and he couldn't stop himself from mentally exploring how he'd noticed her dress and the feel of the curve of her hip when he'd cupped his hand around it earlier.

And she may not have given anything to the kiss, but that didn't stop Ryan from thinking about a do-over.

He cleared his throat. He wished he could clear his mind as easily.

"I'd been thinking the same thing about Pops."

That wasn't all he'd been thinking about. But he wasn't about to tell her that, even if it took every last bit of professional skill to keep it to himself. He'd be honest with her about the gold digger thoughts.

But not these.

"Well, so what do we do?" Lisa shivered as a breeze blew across the sidewalk. Her slim arms flared with goose flesh.

"I'm not sure what we do about our two lovebirds right now." Ryan took off his jacket and with a smooth motion, laid it over Lisa's shoulders. "But I do know we're going to get you inside and get you warm."

"That's okay. I should probably be getting back to Nana."

Ryan smiled. "I wouldn't if I were you. Pops texted me just a few minutes ago and told me they were listening to music clips to decide what they wanted to play at the ceremony."

"It's close to midnight. Nana's never awake this late."

"No one sleeps in Vegas, Lisa. Come on, let's get you inside."

NO FEWER THAN TEN PEOPLE stopped Ryan as they walked back into the hotel. Lisa couldn't believe how everyone seemed to know him. Everyone wanted to talk to "Lucky Charm." And most of them congratulated her, too.

Ryan handled them all deftly. He thanked them for their well-wishes and made practiced small talk as they walked the broad, gilded hallways of the Renaissance Grand.

During her time in New York, a few people recognized her from plays and would stop her on the streets to say something, but Lisa figured the total number of random admirers from her all of her acting days combined came in far fewer than the number of people who stopped Ryan McBride in the last ten minutes.

He was a rock star in this town.

And by being with him, she suddenly became one too. If she'd ever been lucky enough to walk a bonafide red carpet in her brief career as an actress, Lisa imagined it might have felt something like this—hot date and everything.

Lisa did a mental double-take. She needed to focus on the end goal—getting back home with Nana as soon as possible, and keeping her great-grandmother unmarried. Now that she knew she and Ryan felt similarly about their grandparents' plans, Lisa thought it would be easier to achieve her goals. She had someone on her side.

But that was it.

Ryan McBride was just a man in a similar situation. He was also taciturn, impulsive—as evidenced by his little stunt with the TV reporter—and used to getting his own way. It didn't matter if she found him attractive or not because the rest of those qualities added up to trouble in her book.

She tried to stay away from people who kept secrets or didn't think through their actions. She'd seen enough of both during her time in New York. And as a teacher, she always tried to teach her students to act responsibly, and she tried to model that behavior for them.

Which was why she was in Las Vegas—trying to keep Nana from making a decision she clearly hadn't thought through. Or maybe it was, as Lisa suspected, more that Nana couldn't clearly think through the implications of such a complex decision any longer.

And to do what she'd set out to do, Lisa herself would have to keep thinking clearly.

Which meant no more daydreams about Mr. Ryan "Lucky Charm" McBride. Or his dark blue eyes. Or that slightly-more-than-five-o'-clock shadow that gave his face a magnetic edge.

"Lisa?"

He'd caught her staring. So much for that resolution to not notice or care.

"Hmm?" Maybe if she played it cool, he wouldn't pick up on her train of thought.

Oh, who was she kidding? The man played poker for a living. He was trained to pick up on the signals of others and not give away anything in return.

"I thought we could just duck in here and get away from everyone." He nodded at a black lacquered set of double doors. A large man in a black T-shirt tucked into black pants stood in front of the door handles.

Maybe he hadn't noticed anything. "Sure. Lead the way."

"Lucky Charm. Everyone's talking about your big announcement." The man at the door held one open for Lisa and Ryan. "You're not moving away too, are you?"

Ryan put a hand lightly on the small of Lisa's back, guiding her through the entry. She could feel the press of his fingertips and remembered back a few hours to when he'd pulled her close and kissed her twice.

"I don't think so, Mathias. But I honestly don't know. I haven't made any plans yet. Just needed a change."

Ryan talked quietly to a buxom bright redhead just inside the door. "Right this way, Lucky Charm."

She led them around the perimeter of the club and to an area partitioned off on the left side. She pointed at a high-walled booth of quilted leather that had a great view of the two baby grand pianos on a polished stage.

"I'll be right back with your usual, Lucky Charm. What about for your fiancée?"

Word traveled fast. They'd even heard in the clubs. "Um, I don't know. Maybe a Cosmopolitan?"

The waitress adjusted her stick-straight waterfall of hair over her shoulder. "Sure thing. Be right back with your order."

Lisa slid into the well-appointed booth and scooted halfway around. Ryan followed and sat about a foot away, close enough that no one would question the distance between him and his "fiancée," but still far enough to give them both their personal space.

The low sounds of conversation in the nightclub buzzed all around them. Lisa didn't know exactly where they were, but she was always comfortable at the sight of a piano on a stage.

They sat for a second, content to let the sounds of others' conversation fill in the spaces around them. Finally, they both spoke at once.

"Go ahead," Ryan said. A smile tugged at the edge of his lips and Lisa could see the gleam of bright white teeth in the glow of the low, red candle on the table in front of them.

Lisa laid her hands on the table in front of her and clasped them together. "You said you didn't know what you were doing next. Is that true?"

Ryan nodded. "Yeah, it is. Sounds a little crazy, doesn't it? Quitting a job without having another."

"I'd say yes, but I did something similar when I left New York, so I'm probably one of the few people who won't question your plan."

"Or lack thereof." His smile blossomed into a full grin. "Last year, after I won the ring, it just didn't do anything for me. I mean, it was this huge professional accomplishment, but I didn't care. And I started to wonder why. Eventually, as I thought about it, I realized the challenge was gone."

He looked away from Lisa and watched the flame over the candle shimmer.

"Why did you leave New York, Lisa?"

She let out a long sigh. "It's hard to explain. I wasn't like you—I'd gotten some decent roles in some smaller productions and a couple of parts on Broadway, even—including two pretty big understudy roles—you'd know the shows. But I hadn't 'made it.' I wasn't anywhere close. And somewhere along the way, the constant pursuit of success—whatever that was—got tiring. One day, I realized that getting a leading role on a big stage wasn't going to make me somebody. I wasn't going to be somebody unless I was invested in someone's life. And New York is a lonely place for making real connections like that."

The VIP hostess placed a short, slightly curved glass in front of Ryan. The two perfectly square ice cubes clinked as she sat the glass on the table. "Glenmorangie Quinta Ruban. Your favorite." She sat a full bottle in front of the glass and opened it.

She turned to Lisa and took the Cosmopolitan off the tray and placed it delicately on the table. One solitary strip of corkscrew-shaped orange rind floated atop the pink liquid in the distinct, funnel-shaped glass. "And this is for you. Is there anything else I can bring you right now?"

"I don't think so, Anya." Ryan reached for the bottle, then poured a scant amount over the ice.

"I tended bar for a bit in New York to make ends meet, but I'm not sure I've heard of that particular scotch."

"The Quinta Ruban is a limited edition. They keep it here for me. It's aged traditionally, then transferred to Portuguese Madeira pipes. It has a very unique flavor—hints of chocolate and mint, along with some orange, in the finish."

"Oh, so it's like dessert?"

Ryan's eyebrow rose slightly, making him look equal parts rugged and dangerous. "You could say that. If you like your desserts potent."

Lisa's mouth went as dry as if she, herself, had indulged in a glass of whisky, neat. She grabbed the stem of the martini glass and took a long sip of the Cosmo as she counted to herself.

One hippopotamus.

Two hippopotamus.

Three hippopotamus.

Slowly, the potami helped her remember to breathe and her equilibrium righted itself. She put the glass back on the napkin.

"So, back to the earlier conversation. You decided to leave New York because you were lonely?"

She looked away for a second, seeing in her mind's eye the subway ride and the moment it all clicked for her.

"No, not lonely. Just unfulfilled. A friend had gone back to school to get her teaching certificate and was loving working with kids. I thought back on the biggest influences in my life, and aside from Nana, they'd been my teachers. They'd taught me to dream and they'd helped prepare me for the world. I knew I wanted to be that kind of influence on someone." She paused and took another sip of her drink. "So, I bought a one-way ticket home."

"And have you ever regretted it?" Ryan's blue eyes focused on Lisa with laser-like precision.

She could feel the weight of his stare. It was as though he was challenging her to drop all the games they'd played since the moment they'd met and to be completely honest with him. She felt like this was an answer he'd been searching his own heart and mind for.

"Not for one second," Lisa answered honestly. "Well, not until I realized today I couldn't buy a dress in that boutique. Teaching does have some drawbacks."

She tried to smile and make the words seem like more of a joke. She didn't want to be too serious.

"I don't need money. I just need to find something that has a purpose. You've found that. I'd like to do the same."

He sounded sincere. However, Lisa had already learned one thing—Ryan McBride was a professional gambler. He could conceal his real thoughts and move situations to his advantage. He'd kiss a near-stranger on TV and pass her off as his fiancée if it gave him an edge.

But something in the tone of his voice made Lisa turn and look at him more closely, to see if this was just another game to him, or something more.

"Why don't you?"

"Teach?" She could hear the laugh behind his words over the buzz of the crowd.

Clearly, she'd judged him correctly the first time. She kicked herself for not keeping her mouth shut.

She almost didn't know how to respond. She decided to do what she thought Ryan would do in this situation—deflect and move on. "Never mind."

He picked up the cut crystal and swirled the brown liquid around the melting ice cubes. "It's an interesting idea, but I don't know what I'd teach or where I'd go. It's not like Mensa is recruiting me."

"I teach theatre, remember, not nuclear physics. Kids have all types of interests, and they need all types of teachers."

Ryan took a neat sip from the glass. "True. But I doubt there are many parents wanting their kids to learn from a card shark."

"Do you have a college degree?"

"Of course I do. Do you think Pops would have it any other way?" His blue eyes sparkled in a way similar to his grandfather's. "It's in accounting, actually. Math is easy for me. I think it's what's made me a good card player. People think it's all about luck, but really, that's just short-term variance. It comes down to statistics. There are pot odds and implied odds, and you need to know your expected value. If I'm staring someone down during a game, I'm really not looking at them. I'm running all the numbers and scenarios in my head. The best competitive advantage I have isn't that I can read people or keep them from reading me. It's that I'm good at math and I can do fairly detailed calculations in my head during the downtime."

Lisa finished off her Cosmopolitan with a dainty sip. "So, could you teach kids about statistics?"

He shrugged. "I suppose I could."

"I have a co-worker who is one of the curriculum leads for our district's new STEM Academy. It's a school dedicated to teaching Science, Technology, Engineering, and Math. There are ways for you to get a teaching certificate without having an education degree. That's how I did it. You might even qualify for an emergency certificate, depending on how pressed they are for the right skill set. Good math teachers are really hard to find."

"You're serious?" His eyebrow cocked gently again, as though he couldn't quite believe what Lisa was saying.

She nodded. "Of course I am."

Two men walked out on the stage at the front of the room. As they took their places beside their respective pianos, the crowd broke out in wild applause.

Lisa couldn't quite hear what Ryan said in reply, and as the performers began to speak and explain how the dueling piano show worked, there wasn't really a way for her to ask him to repeat himself.

So, she settled back in the tufted booth and tried to focus on the show and not Ryan McBride. It only took a few minutes to realize she wasn't making good on that goal.

She'd thought they'd had nothing in common—the underpaid teacher and the man who tossed the exclusive credit card around without hesitation. But she knew the struggle he was going through, felt it in her veins. She'd lived coming face-to-face with the realization that your life-long dream wasn't enough to make it in real life. She'd walked away from the lights and the stage in search of fulfillment and life's work that would make a difference—without losing the passion she'd loved since childhood.

Ryan was trying to navigate his way through that reality now, staring the unknown in the face and trying to make sense of it. Beyond that, they were both obviously devoted to their respective grandparents and wanted to protect them and care for them.

She tried to turn her head as unobtrusively as possible and look at Ryan's profile. Rich brown hair that was almost raven-black in most light, perfectly styled with just a little bit of bad-boy tousle. Straight nose, strong jawline covered in short stubble that would have been perfect on a motorcycle-riding hero on the big screen.

She let her gaze trace back up. And those eyes. A shred of light from the candle in front of them reflected the deep blue back at her.

She didn't know the full history of that Lucky Charm nickname, but to say that he was charming to look at was probably a solid understatement.

The player on the left piano finished the rendition of "Crocodile Rock" with a resounding crash and a zip of fingers down the full length of the keyboard and back.

"It's always fun to play for a crowd like this, but part of the way we keep the show fun is to bring up people from the audience to join us," the player, who'd earlier introduced himself as Einstein, said to the full house.

His co-performer, a woman who'd introduced herself as Marie, nodded. "Sometimes we take volunteers. Sometimes we pick on people. Tonight, we're picking on people."

Einstein pounded out the theme from *Jaws*. The overhead spotlights began to swirl around the crowd.

"And tonight...we're picking on a man who's creating a little bit of a buzz around town. Ryan McBride, the most decorated winner in Global Poker Challenge history, announced tonight that he's retiring from the tour." Marie's smile was more of a leer. She pointed at Ryan with both fingers in a *pow-pow* motion. "Come on, Lucky Charm, it's time to do your swan song."

Ryan sat up a little straighter and Lisa noticed the tension coming back in his shoulders. He waved his hands in a crossing fashion. "No, no, that's okay. I'm just here to enjoy the show."

Even sitting next to him, Lisa had a hard time hearing his denial, so she was certain Marie hadn't heard it up on the elevated stage area. But clearly, she'd picked up the gist of the message.

She slid off her bench and walked with determination in sky-high black patent heels down the center stairs. The bright lights overhead swept down the path between the tables and landed squarely on the curved booth where Lisa and Ryan had both been comfortably incognito only moments before.

"Every single time," Ryan muttered, and this time, Lisa heard the words clearly as he spat them out under his breath.

Marie stretched out her hand. "I think we also all owe you congratulations on your upcoming wedding. When's the big day?"

Lisa kept her eyes on Ryan, studying his reaction. He looked...exhausted wasn't quite the right word, but it was close. There was a hollowness that crept over his features with every step closer of Marie's.

"We haven't decided." Lisa jumped in. Ryan had brought her here as a nice gesture to her, to keep her out of the way of the real engaged couple in both their lives. Deflecting some of the spotlight's glare was the least she could do.

He reached over, protected from Marie's eyes by the overhang of the table, and gave Lisa's hand a small squeeze. The simple gesture surprised Lisa. When he didn't pull his hand away, it surprised Lisa even more that the lingering contact didn't bother her.

"Well, it's Vegas! No planning necessary. There's a chapel on every corner." Marie turned and looked at the audience knowingly. "Raise your hand, folks. Who's gotten married in Vegas?"

A number of hands raised. Einstein played an up-tempo version of the traditional bridal chorus.

"How many of you are still married to that person?" Marie chuckled as she asked. A few of the hands lowered.

"See? It's not that hard, Lucky Charm. Einstein's even got a copy of the marriage license form over there. We keep them for special occasions. The Bureau is still open. You could make an honest woman of her tonight. All you need is sixty dollars in cash to get this processed."

Einstein picked up a form out of a basket on the table next to him and waved it to emphasize the point, then went back to playing Mendelssohn's best-known tune.

"Marie." Ryan bit out the words, not wanting to play along any further. "I don't carry cash."

The dueling piano diva was undeterred. She'd hooked herself a prize and wanted to continue riding this as long as she could. The audience was eating her banter up, much to Lisa's chagrin. She hoped her cheeks weren't starting to flush.

"Pass the bucket, Einstein!" Marie waved in her partner's direction and shouted. "We do this all the time. No worries at all, Lucky Charm. We've got you covered."

Ryan leaned forward, his posture clearly becoming more defensive as people began tossing dollars in the cheap plastic bucket Einstein had tossed into the crowd. "Marie, I'm sure these people came here for a musical show, not a matrimonial one. Let's get back to the music, shall we?"

He spoke with a razor-sharp edge that left little room for contradicting him. Marie shrugged.

"Well, there is one way to get me to stop being your wedding planner."

"Name it." There was steel in each syllable.

"Come on stage and sing." Marie turned back to the crowd and waved her handheld microphone.

"I don't sing." Ryan tugged on Lisa's hand and moved out of the booth. "Come on, Lisa. It's time to find something else to do."

Marie paused, apparently thinking of some retort. Lisa cringed. She didn't want this comedy routine at Ryan's expense to continue. But she also didn't think leaving was the right answer. If he walked out now, he'd look like a bad sport. And he was well-known enough around here that word would spread like wildfire. Look how many people thought he was engaged.

She figured that Ryan probably wouldn't care if people talked about him. But tomorrow started the last tournament of his career. She remembered leaving New York abruptly and hearing the rumors others started about her.

Lisa had never regretted leaving the bright lights and the big city, but she had regretted how people in her circle reacted to her decision.

Ryan deserved to end his poker days on his terms at the table. Not with everyone whispering behind his back about what a bad sport he was and how he couldn't take a joke.

The words leaped out of her mouth almost as soon as she realized she could take some of the pressure off him. "I can sing."

"What?" Ryan's voice sounded harsh as gravel and his eyes narrowed as they locked on hers.

"I can sing. I'm classically trained. I was in the cast of several large musicals on Broadway. This is my thing."

"Lisa, we can just go." Ryan lowered his voice and the rough sound smoothed out.

He'd bought her this dress so she could go to her beloved great-grandmother's engagement dinner. He'd set up that engagement dinner and picked up the tab even when he suspected that she and Nana were just here to take advantage of the grandfather that he loved dearly. And he'd done it all, in spite of believing the wedding shouldn't even happen.

When he spoke, he was blunt. When he was silent, he had an uncanny ability to conceal his thoughts. When he thought someone was being a fool, he didn't suffer them lightly.

And when she'd seen a glimpse of the passions that drove him and the heart he had for his family, they'd been as limitless as that high-end credit card in his back pocket.

As soon as she met him, Lisa Fleming had figured out that Ryan McBride was infuriating.

But she'd also seen that he had a heart of gold. And because of that, she wanted to do something in return for him.

"Come on." She put out her hand and waited, holding her breath, until Ryan laid his hand across her palm. "It'll be fun."

Chapter Five

RYAN HAD SAT ON A BARSTOOL for thirty minutes, mesmerized by the way Lisa handled the crowd. She was a seasoned professional. He could also clearly see that the confident, sexy woman who'd walked out of the honeymoon suite bathroom and down to dinner with him earlier was some enhanced version of Lisa.

Not enhanced in a fake or off-putting way, but amplified. It was as though when she stepped on a stage, she plugged in, like a sparkling strand of twinkle lights at Christmas. Being in front of an audience made her come alive.

Once Marie and Einstein found out which shows she'd been in on Broadway, they started cueing up show tunes, one after another. Lisa belted them out with polished precision and Ryan found himself content to sit on the edge and just watch her weave her spell.

Normally, he worked so hard to control a situation, to analyze the odds and work the scenarios in his favor.

For once in his life, he was able to slow down and just be.

For once in his life, he wasn't wishing for more.

For once in his life, all eyes weren't on him. But his eyes were locked on Lisa.

Anya had tiptoed on stage a few minutes ago and handed him a refill. Ryan sipped the unique scotch thoughtfully. The

Glenmorangie Quinta Ruban would surprise any scotch drinker. In a glass, it looked like any other scotch whisky, clear and the color of burnished honey—the same color of Lisa Fleming's eyes and the curls that escaped the neat twist of her formal occasion hairstyle.

But one sip of the Quinta Ruban, with the light, sweet notes aged into it, would tell even the most casual of scotch drinkers that it was out of the ordinary.

Much like how one evening with Lisa had changed the opinion he'd formed right off the bat in the baggage claim at the airport. Ryan wasn't necessarily used to being wrong. But for some reason, this time, it felt right to stand corrected.

"Let's hear it for Broadway's own Lisa Fleming!" Marie pushed back the piano bench as she leaped to her feet.

Lisa beamed, but tried to wave off the rolling wave of applause that had brought several members of the audience to their feet as well.

The smile on her face glowed brighter than the spotlight that shone above her. Ryan stood up and joined in the applause. Not just in recognition of the performance she'd given along with Einstein and Marie, but in approval of the real Lisa who was shining through.

She was animated, in charge, and in that lace and feathered number, enough to make him wish she'd kissed him back during that TV stunt earlier—so he wouldn't have any hesitation about doing it again.

But she'd made it clear where she'd stood on that issue, and no matter how much this moment made her come alive—or how looking at her in that dress, listening to her clear, strong voice made certain aspects of his awareness come alive—Ryan had no choice but to respect her on that.

As they stepped off the stage, Ryan leaned close to Lisa and caught a whiff of light floral perfume he hadn't noticed before. "Do you want to stay for the rest of the show, or go somewhere else?"

Lisa raised her arm and looked at the dainty watch circling her wrist. "It's getting late. I wonder if Nana and Bill are finished yet."

Ryan placed his hand at the small of her back and guided her toward the door. "Pops usually has several hours of snoring in a recliner to his credit by this point in any given night. I can't see how he could possibly still be awake."

They wound through the halls and walkways of the Renaissance Grand, toward the main bank of elevators to the rooms. "Do you want me to walk you back to your suite?"

Lisa smoothed at the feathers that floated a few inches above her knee. "I wouldn't want you to go out of your way. You've already done a lot for me today."

"Do you have your keycard? I'll need to swipe it once we get in the elevator." He punched the up button on the dedicated suite elevator. "It's no trouble, I promise. It's a big hotel. I'd hate for you to get lost."

What he'd hate even more, Ryan realized as he took the shiny red card Lisa handed him, was seeing this evening come to an end. For too long, he'd treated this hotel like an office building and the places he had to be seen and events he had to show up to as meetings. The last few hours with Lisa had felt different. For a short, but memorable period, he'd had the chance to see the city as so many tourists did.

The shiny doors opened and they walked out and along the hallway that led to the honeymoon suite Lisa was sharing with her great-grandmother.

Ryan paused before swiping the keycard in the door.

"Thanks again for everything, Ryan. I mean it. You know how I feel about all this wedding nonsense, but you've made it a special day for my Nana. And for today, that's what counts."

Ryan knew he wasn't ready for his Vegas tourist evening to end. He didn't want to be like Cinderella and go back to his cynical, local life. But he also knew he couldn't make a move on her, even though no one else was around to see. He leaned down and gently touched his lips to her cheek, then pulled back and turned to the door so he could swipe the key. He didn't want to see the look on Lisa's face. She'd set boundaries on that sidewalk earlier, and he knew he'd just pushed them—but he didn't want the full confirmation.

The door opened with a click. Lamps glowed in the main living area and the curtains across the back were open to let in the thousands of twinkling lights that packed the Vegas night sky. But everything else in the room was dark and quiet. Even so, it wasn't the dark and quiet of sleep. It was the dark and quiet of empty.

"Nana? Where are you?" Lisa called out as she walked across the room. Clearly, she'd picked up on the vibe as well.

She opened every door in the suite, poking her head in each room and closet.

"Ryan, they're gone," Lisa called from the bedroom. "Nana left me a note."

"They're what?" He walked quickly toward the bedroom and pushed back the door to see Lisa reading a note written in cramped handwriting on a piece of hotel stationery.

"Dear Lisa," she read aloud. "Bill and I had a lovely time planning our big day, but we're so excited we can't sleep. We decided you only get married in Vegas once—at least at our age—and we thought we'd go be tourists. We'll probably be down at the slot machines. Bill said he's going to take me to the buffet too. Don't wait up for me. I'm in good hands. If we need anything, Bill said everyone knows his grandson, so someone will be available to help. We're going on a day trip to Lake Mead tomorrow. You're welcome to come. XOXO Nana. PS, just remember what happens in Vegas stays in Vegas. I think I'm supposed to say that. It's a rule or something."

Lisa lowered her arm and shook her head.

"Slot machines? Buffets? Lakes?"

Ryan could see the edge of the paper wrinkle as Lisa dug her nails into the sheet covering her palm.

"Do you want me to call someone and have them go look for Pops and Gina Mae?"

The lines of worry furrowed deep across Lisa's brow and Ryan wished he could do something to erase them for her. To say she'd had a long day would be an understatement.

"No, not yet. If she's not back in a little bit, I will." She reached back and started pulling out the pins that anchored her twist of hair. She placed the pins in a pile at the edge of the dresser to her right, then ran her hands under her hair and fluffed out the curls and tangles. "I don't know what to think, Ryan. This isn't like her. I really am going to need to call her doctor in the morning and make an appointment. It scares me to think that something's truly wrong, but I don't have any other explanations."

"I'll wait with you if you want. Come on, let's go sit in the living room. Maybe we can find a movie on TV or something."

She walked toward the door, then stopped. "You really don't have to. You've got that tournament tomorrow."

"It starts at ten. I have to be there a little early to do my buy-in and get settled, but I'll be fine. I've done all this before. It's routine."

Lisa threaded her fingers in her hair again. "I'm not sure what's given me this headache—my hair pulled back like that, the Cosmopolitan, or Nana. Maybe it's all three. Either way, I think I need to change out of this dress and heels and try and be a little more comfortable. Do you mind giving me a minute?"

Ryan tried to keep every clichéd thought out of his mind when she mentioned slipping into something more comfortable. What happened in Vegas, as Gina Mae pointed out, was indeed supposed to stay in Vegas. But that rule was probably not coined with one's future step-something-or-other in mind.

And he knew he'd do well to keep that fact in his consciousness instead of keeping that dress and her pitch-perfect voice at the top of his train of thought. If they weren't successful in keeping Pops and Gina Mae from walking down the little white chapel aisle, Ryan and Lisa would likely be seeing more of each other in the years to come. Letting his thoughts wander right now would only make Thanksgiving and Christmas awkward.

"Sure. I'll go check what's on TV." Ryan walked back to the living room, but stopped at the phone on a side table and punched in five numbers.

"VIP Concierge Desk, Winter speaking. How may I help you?"

"Hi, Winter. It's Ryan McBride. Listen, I need your help with something."

"Certainly, Mr. McBride."

Ryan tried to keep his voice down. He knew Lisa had told him not to call, but he was just as concerned about Pops as she was about her nana. There wasn't any harm in having someone check. There were thousands of cameras in this casino. A welfare check could be done quickly and efficiently.

"My grandfather left a note that he and his..." Ryan paused. "Well, his fiancée, left a note that they were going to the slots and the buffet. Can someone check on them for me? It's late and I just want to make sure everything's okay."

"Certainly, Mr. McBride. I'll make a few calls and then I'll let you know."

Ryan pushed his left shoe off with the toe of his right shoe. Lisa wasn't the only one who felt confined. "Thanks. And can you send some sparkling water and cheese and fruit up as well?"

"Certainly, Mr. McBride. You're not calling from your penthouse, though. Am I sending it to Mrs. Fleming's suite?"

"Yes. I'll be in here for the time being. Until we get everything settled with my grandfather."

"Very good, Mr. McBride. I'll have everything taken care of for you."

"Thanks, Winter."

Ryan hung up the phone, freed his other foot from the Italian leather shoe, and took off his sport coat, then laid it carefully across the back of the closest chair.

He was sitting on the couch, flipping through the channels on the flat-screen TV mounted to the wall, when Lisa came out.

Ryan stifled a laugh as he looked up. Lisa acknowledged Ryan's expression, then sashayed across the marble flooring. The gentle tilt of her hips as she walked made him forget all about the crazy get-up she was sporting.

"I told you Nana packed my suitcase. Apparently, she's forgotten where I keep my pajamas because she packed this rockin' number for me. Like it?"

She looked as though she were barely holding in her own laughter. Clad in a lightweight cotton nightdress made out of white fabric with a yellow buttercup motif, it was accentuated—if you could really call it that—with some old-fashioned lace, yellow ribbon, and a Peter Pan collar.

"As your grandmother so eloquently said, 'what happens in Vegas, stays in Vegas.' I promise I won't tell anyone."

"Thanks." Lisa rolled her eyes a little and landed in the far corner of the couch with a small flop. "I'm pretty sure this is older than me. If I hadn't already decided to call Dr. Reynolds, this would have definitely made up my mind."

"It's...um, fancy. I put on a chick flick. I figured you'd like that best."

"Thanks."

A knock sounded at the door. Lisa popped straight up and out of her lounging position. "Who could that be? I can't answer the door like this." An edge of panic slid into her voice. "Nana should have taken her key."

"It's probably room service. I'll get it."

"I didn't order room service," Lisa said, still pressing back into the cushions as though she wished they'd swallow her and her nightdress whole.

"I did. I thought you might like a snack as you waited up."

Lisa's face relaxed and the corners of her mouth inched up briefly. "Thank you. That was very thoughtful of you."

Ryan walked to the door. "Well, it's easy to pull off when you have twenty-four-seven concierge access. Living attached to a hotel has some perks."

A young man in a starched white jacket brought in a large tray and placed it on the sideboard in the entry. "Winter wanted me to let you know that he spoke with Ray in security. Your grandfather has been playing in the casino for the past hour, but they've just moved to the restaurant."

"Thank you for the tray and the information." Ryan reached into his back pocket and pulled out a handful of bills and offered them to the attendant. Contrary to what he'd told Marie in the nightclub earlier, he always carried cash around. He lived at the Renaissance Grand. There was always someone he needed to tip.

The young man folded the money and stuffed it in the lower pocket of his jacket. "Anything else I can do for you, sir? Can I put the tray in the dining room for you?"

Ryan looked over his shoulder and caught Lisa waving a hand emphatically. "No. I'll take it from here."

As soon as the attendant left, Ryan picked up the tray and placed it on the low table in the center of the living area. He twisted the cap off a bottle of water and handed it to Lisa. "Would you like some ice or a glass?"

"Bottle's fine. I would like one of those strawberries, though. Thanks for checking up on Nana. I know I said not to, but..."

"I wanted to put your mind at ease. And mine too, honestly." Ryan handed her two berries on a napkin, then picked up some grapes for himself and sat back down. "Tell me more about this teaching thing."

Lisa screwed the cap back on her water bottle and placed it on the table. "So you've actually thought about it?"

"I didn't even know something like that existed." He wanted to hear more about the program, but not so much for himself. He wanted to know more about Lisa and he figured this would get her to share more about her own experiences teaching.

He also wondered how he could steer the conversation around to find out if she was single.

Not that it mattered. As soon as the two of them figured out how to talk Pops and Gina Mae out of their wedding, she'd be on the next plane flight back to Texas, and he'd still be here in Nevada, trying to figure out where his luck would take him next.

Lisa told him more about the alternative certification programs and what the kids were like at her high school and what she knew of the vision for the STEM Academy. The light in her eyes as she talked about her students shone almost as brightly as it had when she'd stood in front of a baby grand piano with a spotlight shining down on her.

She clearly cared about her students and the work she was doing. Even at his highest point, Ryan didn't know if he'd loved being on the tour that much. It was challenging and a good way to make a living, but as he'd come to find out, it wasn't a way to really make a difference.

"Tomorrow's tournament is a one-day event to raise money for education, actually."

Lisa reached for another berry. "Really?"

"Yeah, part of everyone's buy-in goes to the pot, but then the rest of the money goes to the Cards for Kids foundation. The Shamrocks for Students tournament helps buy technology for underprivileged schools."

"That sounds like a great cause." Lisa gave a small yawn and Ryan caught his gaze lingering on the circle shape of her mouth. "I didn't know something like that could come out of a poker tournament."

"This is the largest one the Global Poker Challenge does for charity. I won last year."

Lisa stood up and walked to the trash can near the open sliding glass door to throw away her empty water bottle. "When you say you *won*, what exactly does that mean? I don't want to be nosy, but how much does one *win* in a charity poker tournament?"

"Well, last year, there were forty-five players. The buy-in is one million dollars."

She cut his explanation off. "One million dollars? Just to play?"

Ryan nodded. "And the pot was just over forty million."

Lisa stood still as a statue. "You made forty million dollars? In one game?"

"No, I didn't. That was the total pot."

She nodded. "Oh, okay."

"I made just over sixteen million."

Lisa let out a low whistle and turned to face the Vegas skyline. "I take back everything I said about teaching. Stick with poker. Go tell that little reporter it was all a joke."

"Not going to do that. That wasn't the first time I've won an eight-figure pot. What do I need more money for?"

She gave him a laugh over her shoulder. "I don't know. It's not something I've ever had to think about. Maybe you could buy your own private Caribbean island."

"I own a condo on Eleuthera in the Bahamas."

"Of course you do. I stayed at a chain hotel in Biloxi last summer. It's probably about the same."

Even though Lisa's eyes remained fixed on the twinkle of lights and shine of neon below, Ryan knew the way she saw him—really saw him, not just vision—had changed. He could feel it.

"I'd be lying if I said I didn't like the money, Lisa. But everyone makes assumptions because what I earn is a matter of public record. It's splashed on a TV screen if the event's televised, and the big ones I play in now are. But it's not who I am." Ryan walked over to the expanse of glass and nighttime glitter and stopped just over a foot behind Lisa. "It's brought me some nice things, but the most important thing it's brought me is peace of mind. It means I have Pops in the best assisted living facility in this part of the country, and no matter what happens to him between now and Heaven, I can make sure he's taken care of."

"I'm jealous," she whispered.

Ryan leaned forward, trying to hear Lisa.

"I don't have that. I never will. I've spent all day knowing I have to take Nana to Dr. Reynolds when I get her home, but I'm terrified of what he's going to say. What if it is Alzheimer's? Alzheimer's patients require hands-on care. I can't quit my job, but it sure doesn't pay me enough to afford some fancy care facility. And whatever savings Nana planned on having was eaten up when her deadbeat granddaughter dropped me on her doorstep to raise with no additional financial support."

Her story sounded a lot like his own, just with a slightly different ending. He knew about being raised by a grandparent and wanting to provide them the world.

He couldn't give Lisa the world, but maybe he could let her know she wasn't alone. Ryan closed the space between them with one step and put his hands on her shoulders. The cotton and ruffles of the nightdress flattened under his palms. Lisa craned her head slightly and looked back at him.

Gently, he adjusted the pressure on her shoulders and coaxed her to turn toward him. The light glowing behind the waves of her hair, still gently lacquered with a coating of hairspray, gave her a gentle look he didn't get to see often on women in Las Vegas.

There were too many hard people in this town, looking out for the next good time or the next big break. Since the minute Lisa Fleming had walked into Ryan McBride's life, the only thing she'd been looking out for was the woman she called Nana. And she'd just admitted her best wasn't good enough.

"You don't know what the doctor is going to say, Lisa. Don't beat yourself up over something that may not happen."

He lifted a hand and brushed the hair back from her cheek, tucking it behind one ear.

Lisa looked down toward the floor and nodded. "Something's not right. It hasn't been right for a while. I've just chosen to pretend otherwise. She's Nana. I can't even think about something happening to her. She was there for me when no one else—not even my own mother—wanted me. I can't even think about not having her, not having anyone."

"Lisa, you're the kind of person who won't be alone. You're caring, you've got a passion for the kids you teach, you've got a great voice. And you're beautiful."

She rolled her eyes as she looked up at him. "What was in that fancy scotch of yours? Because in case you haven't noticed, I'm wearing some flowered thing from the seventies."

"I don't care what you're wearing. That's not what I'm talking about."

Ryan found his way into territory he hadn't wandered into for a long time. When you went out with models, you didn't usually have to tell them they were beautiful. They heard it every day—they already knew it. And most of the ones he wound up with weren't much for deep conversation anyway.

But Ryan was not about to let Lisa sell herself short. The woman who loved her Nana, who loved her students? She was beautiful in a way that no woman on a catwalk ever could be. But he didn't know which words would be enough to make her believe it.

Again, his fingers stroked the curl he'd tucked behind her ear. Before he'd realized what was happening, his pointer finger traced the edge of her jawline, meeting her soft skin where it curved from her cheek down to her throat.

The soft sound of her breath catching in her throat brought his hand lower, tracing the column of her neck to the space between her collarbones, then following the line of the collarbone back out to her shoulder. Ryan's other hand moved up and settled at the base of her skull.

He could feel her hair thick between his fingers and the side of his hand pressed against the hollow between chin and neck where her heartbeat came rapidly. His own pulse matched hers, beat for staccato beat and he gently tugged with his fingers, tilting her head back and raising her lips to his own.

This time, he wasn't trying to show off.

This time, she kissed back.

This time, all bets were off as the first tentative moments of touch gave way to a more realistic exploration of the moment.

Ryan gave what momentary security he could to Lisa, and she leaned in, laying her forearms over his shoulders and taking the sanctuary offered. She might have been a trained actress, but there was no pretense between them as she moved as close to him as the folds of floral cotton and lace would allow.

A loud plastic scratch sounded in the distance. Lisa jumped back at the sound of the keycard in the door.

She smoothed a hand over her hair, unruly from Ryan's exploration. "Oh my goodness, what would Nana have said if she'd walked in on that?"

Ryan tried to force his breathing to slow and take his pounding heart with it. He grinned, almost as much at the thought of getting caught by two Social Security chaperones as he was from the memory of the soft exploration of Lisa's mouth, and his hands roaming the curves of her body as they were guarded by shapeless cotton.

"I don't know what your Nana would say, but I'm pretty sure Pops would have given me two thumbs up."

Chapter Six

THE TRIP TO LAKE MEAD had been moved to after lunch, thanks to Nana's big night out with Bill. The two grandparents had returned from their slot machine and buffet date night and not even batted an eye at Lisa and Ryan waiting together for their return. They'd said hi, Pops had given Nana a good night kiss, and Nana had trotted off to bed without any further word.

Ryan told Lisa good night—words only, no more kissing—and said he would escort Pops back to his room on the next floor down. Before she knew it, Lisa stood alone in the expansive suite, and within a few minutes, she could hear soft snoring coming from Nana's room.

At least someone in the suite could sleep. Lisa sure couldn't. She'd tossed and turned, thinking of how Ryan had turned her in his arms and how her heart rate had gotten tossed into the stratosphere the moment his lips touched hers.

This kiss had been so different from the one for the TV cameras. That had been a stunt, a joke. But alone, with the lights of Vegas spilling a glow across the living room of the suite, no one had been laughing.

And then Lisa'd spent all night reliving it. By the time the sun started to glow through the crack in the curtains, she gave up, called room service, and ordered a croissant with chocolate hazelnut spread and a full carafe of very strong coffee.

By her fourth cup of coffee, she started to wake up and as she pulled the front section of hair off her face and secured it with a clip, she couldn't help but compare the buzz from the coffee off the buzz she'd gotten from the kiss with Ryan.

"What a mess," she muttered to her reflection in the mirror.

"What mess?" Nana padded into the bathroom, brow furrowed as she scanned the room in search of something. "Have you seen my toothpaste? I can't find it and I need minty fresh breath for today."

Lisa stuck her hand in her travel bag of toiletries. "Here, use mine. You've renewed your commitment to dental hygiene?"

Nana nodded and grinned. "Bill says my smile reminds him of when we were eighteen. He says it hasn't changed a bit."

"I can't argue with that, Nana. You've always had a beautiful smile." Lisa went back to brushing her hair.

Nana stepped over to the second sink and turned on the tap. "You have the same smile, girlie. But it's hiding today. Don't you know this is the happiest place on earth?"

"That's Disneyland, Nana. Head a few hours to the west. This is Las Vegas. Sin City."

"Whmpmvr." Her response was muffled by the suds and bubbles covering her teeth. She spit the toothpaste in the sink, picked up a glass, and rinsed. "It's *my* happiest place on earth. And tomorrow is my wedding day!"

Even though Lisa's misgivings about Nana's impending wedding loomed as high as the mountains in the Nevada desert around them, there was no denying the joy in Nana's voice. She hadn't heard that simple happiness in a while. The sweet sound lightened Lisa's heart.

"But something's bothering you, my dear. I can tell. What is it?"

Lisa tried to wave off Nana's concern. She wasn't even sure Nana would really understand. "It's nothing."

"Yes, it is. Don't lie to me, Lisa Marie."

Lisa leaned forward and watched carefully in the mirror as she applied her lipstick. She took more time than usual, trying to decide what she would say to Nana.

"I wasn't lying, Nana, not really. It's just...well...it's Ryan McBride. But it's really nothing."

"Bill says Ryan's unhappy." Nana reached out her hand. "Let me use your lipstick, dearie."

Lisa laughed a little bit. "I guess so. He quit his job yesterday."

Nana puckered her lips into an O and dotted the lipstick around, then smoothed it out by pressing her lips together. Just the same way she'd done it Lisa's whole life. "I'd heard his name mentioned by a lot of people downstairs last night, but I didn't know what they were talking about."

"He announced on TV that he was leaving the Global Poker Challenge tour."

"Yes, but people were saying something else too." Nana handed the lipstick back to Lisa, then shrugged. "But I can't remember. I wonder what it was."

"That he was engaged?" Lisa went with the most obvious choice.

"Yes! That's it. He was engaged." Nana's eyes sparkled a bit. "I love weddings. I hope he invites Bill and me. Did he say who he was marrying?"

Lisa took a deep breath. "You're not getting an invitation, Nana."

"And why not? I'm marrying his grandfather."

Lisa wanted to laugh at the indignation in Nana's voice over the perceived slight.

"Because there's no wedding."

"Lisa Marie, you're really confusing me. Why would people be saying he was getting married if there was no wedding? Did it already happen?"

"No. It's just not going to happen." For the life of her, Lisa had no idea how to explain this one.

Nana raised her eyebrow. She was not dropping this until the answers made sense to her. "And why not?"

May as well just throw it out there. The whole thing was confusing anyway, potential Alzheimer's or not.

"Because the people who were talking think I'm Ryan's fiancée."

Nana's smile returned to her face with a wattage to rival the brightest Vegas neon. "Oh, how wonderful! We can have a double wedding!"

Lisa opened her mouth to try and explain better, then she shut it abruptly. She couldn't take that smile off Nana's face. She just couldn't.

She just raised her hands, covered her face, and tried not to think about kissing the man Nana now thought was her fiancé.

THE FIRST FEW ROUNDS of poker tournaments like this always went slowly, as they narrowed the ranks. Ryan knew it was unprofessional, but he couldn't keep his thoughts on the game. They kept coming back to Lisa and that kiss.

He'd first run his mind over the kisses they'd shared in this room yesterday, while the NCN cameras rolled.

But he didn't care to focus on those for very long.

He didn't care to focus on his cards.

He just wanted to think about the sweet surrender he tasted in the suite last night when Lisa kissed him back as the lights of Vegas glowed behind them.

Snap out of it. You've got business to take care of. You're going out after this. You need to go out on top.

As another round of cards was dealt, Ryan looked at the back of the room.

A familiar white-haired man in a seersucker suit came in the room, wearing the VIP pass Ryan had left for him. To his right was another cotton-topped VIP, dressed in an oversized floral print blouse and pants that appeared to be of a sturdy, thick knit. She'd put on her pearls for the occasion, Ryan noted, and wore her VIP pass like another necklace.

Behind them came the face he'd thought about all morning.

Lisa didn't look left or right, just slightly down, as she followed straight behind her great-grandmother and her great-grandmother's fiancé. The loose waves of her hair tumbled like a honey-and-cinnamon waterfall and partly obscured the gentle features of her face.

Ryan leaned back in his chair and squinted. He wished he'd been able to see her lips. Maybe, like finally hearing an earworm tune, just a small glimpse of her mouth would put an end to the revolving kiss-cam in his mind.

The small group followed the GPC staffer to three empty seats. Of course, they were in front. Of course, they were near his table. The young man probably thought he was doing his job well to sit Ryan's VIPs down by him.

Usually, it was good to have Pops in the audience. Pops had taught him his first lessons on cards so many years ago, and having his steady, supportive presence nearby always seemed to bring him a certain amount of luck. Even though the poker world knew Ryan himself as the "Lucky Charm," Ryan always thought of Pops as his personal secret weapon—the real lucky charm.

But today, Pops brought baggage. Specifically, a fiancée who may or may not have a soon-to-be-evaluated dementia issue and the great-granddaughter who worried about her—and who, in turn, Ryan found himself worrying about.

When they called a break in between rounds, Pops stood up and walked over to the rail closest to Ryan.

"We're about to head out to Lake Mead, son."

"Okay, Pops." Ryan looked just past his grandfather to the two women with him. "Is everyone going?"

Pops nodded. "Everyone but you. Gina Mae and Lisa are both coming along. Your concierge friend called me this morning and said the car would be here around one-thirty.

We'll go see the lake and have dinner. Looks like you'll be here late tonight."

"That's always the goal."

"Last man standing." Pops gave him a confident smile. "I know this is your last tournament. I just wanted to say how proud of you I am, son. I know people think poker is just a game. But you found something you loved a long time ago and you worked hard to be the best. It's paid off in a way I never thought possible when I pulled out that first deck of cards when you were a kid. I just thought it would be something we could play together after dinner—a way to connect with a scared little boy who'd been through a lot of changes. I don't know what you'll do after you leave this room for good, Ryan McBride, but I know you'll be successful. And I hope you know I'll always be proud of you."

Pops clapped a hand around Ryan's bicep once, then twice. Ryan felt his throat constrict with memories. And love. For more years than he could count, Bill McBride had been his whole world. He'd stood in as mother, father, grandparent, confidante, mentor...and friend.

Ryan loved the man more than words could ever say.

He'd tried to repay Pops by making sure he was cared for. That he had the best housing and assistance money could buy. That he didn't have to work or worry. That after a lifetime of seeing to it that Ryan had comfort and security in his life—when he'd started out with so little of both—Pops could now enjoy both of those necessities for the rest of the days the good Lord gave him on Earth.

But as he stood there, staring into Bill's icy-blue eyes and seeing love and pride shining back in their reflection, Ryan was hit with a gut punch more solid than a prize fighter's knockout blow. Money hadn't been what made Pops—and the memories he'd created—special for Ryan. Pops had worked for years after his retirement age to support the child who came under his roof long after his contemporaries sported empty nests.

Time, love, and personal interest had been the tools Pops used.

And Ryan could give Pops all the money and assisted living in the world, but he couldn't give him twenty-four-seven companionship.

But that sweet woman who walked into Pops' open arms at McCarron International Airport yesterday could.

Ryan shifted his gaze from Pops to Lisa, speaking in slow, hushed tones to her grandmother. Although he and Lisa had just met, she'd felt comfortable enough with Ryan to confide her fears about her great-grandmother's health. Ryan didn't want to betray that trust.

The more he thought about it though, following through on his original gut instinct—preventing the marriage from happening—would be a betrayal of the lifetime of support Pops had given him.

However, he knew that Lisa had a similar connection to her great-grandmother, and she was opposing Nana's trip down the aisle for very real, valid reasons—ones he'd shared until this very moment.

Ryan knew he was stuck between a rock and a hard place.

He also knew that he had a game to play, business to attend to. He needed to clear this lump in his throat and the thoughts in his head, then get back to the table, and get his mind focused.

Ryan put his hand on Pops' shoulder, mirroring the reassuring gesture Pops had given him.

"I love you, Pops. You know that, right?"

"Of course I do, son. I told you yesterday that you had a cynic's heart. That's not quite right—you have a cautious heart." Pops smiled, pushing away the thick fog in Ryan's brain as the corners of his mouth raised. "I hope that once you're out of this business you can have an open one. Life's too short to not take chances. I could have married Gina Mae more than six decades ago in a quickie wedding at the courthouse. I don't regret marrying your Memaw or having you in my life. But now, my greatest wish is for you to be happy, son, and to not live with what-ifs. But I know you're going to have to take a chance and see what it's like on the other side, the less cautious side, to get there. Now, son...get back to that table and go out in style."

Ryan walked to the spot they'd set up for him for this next round of the tournament. He saw Pops talking with Gina Mae and Lisa and gesturing toward the door. He figured they were discussing the Town Car which would be arriving soon at the hotel's front door to take them on a sunny day of Nevada sightseeing.

They rose and headed for the doors at the back of the room. Ryan sat in his chair and studied them carefully.

He didn't want to be stuck inside these four walls, overanalyzing facial tics and mentally counting cards round after round after round. He was quitting the game because he'd grown bored with the rote, with the predictability of the tasks. He'd mastered the skill and now it did come down to luck.

But he didn't want to be lucky at cards anymore.

He wanted to be lucky in life.

Pops was right. Ryan needed to see a side of life where every move wasn't calculated and evaluated against the decisions of others and the whims of rectangles with royal designs printed on them.

Lisa turned her head as she paused at the door. She looked at the spot where Ryan had been sitting in the last round, then scanned the other tables in the room. She didn't see him at his new corner table, and it gave him a moment to watch her.

Ryan knew Lisa was looking for him.

Pops had been looking for Gina Mae.

Who was he looking for?

He'd been looking out for just himself for far too long.

The other players filed back to the tables and took their places for the next round of the tournament, scheduled to begin shortly. Ryan looked at his watch and watched a handful of seconds tick away.

He looked up and no one stood near the back door. Lisa was gone.

The wave of adrenaline and pure physical desire that had overpowered him last night when he'd put his hands on Lisa's shoulders to give her some support and let her know she wasn't alone—it returned with the force of a gale.

"So, I guess this may be the last time we sit down at a table together, LC." Davian Rentfrow took the seat next to him. "It's been good playing you, man. Good luck in retirement."

Even though Davian had always been a good guy and a worthy challenger, Ryan couldn't even look toward him in acknowledgment.

"Thanks, man," he said, acutely aware of the absent tone in his voice, but unable to do anything about it.

Go out in style. Pops' last words before he left with Gina Mae and Lisa hung in Ryan's mind.

The outcome of this tournament didn't change anything for him. He had a lifetime of money, and then some. He'd already announced his retirement—nothing depended on how he fared in this game. And the charity already got his buy-in.

He didn't win anything he needed by staying, and he didn't lose anything of value by going.

Ryan stood up and pushed his chair back from the table. He walked over to a tournament official and muttered a few sentences in his ear, then he headed for the door between the playing floor and the viewing area.

Emma, the NCN reporter, tried to block his path.

"Where are you headed, Lucky Charm?" She pushed her microphone close to his face, but Ryan batted it away with one swat.

"I'm going all in, Emma." He edged through the door and around her attempts to block him. "And the name's not Lucky Charm. It's Ryan. Just Ryan."

LISA LOOKED AT THE sleek, black car in the circular drive of the hotel. She knew the cliché said everything was bigger in Texas, but apparently, it applied to Las Vegas too. Bill had told her over lunch that Ryan had arranged for a Town Car to drive them out to Lake Mead. Clearly, they watered and fertilized their Town Cars in Vegas, because where Lisa came from, this car was called a limousine.

"The hotel upgraded your car, Mr. McBride, with our compliments on your upcoming wedding to Mrs. Fleming, sir." The head bellhop opened the door to the passenger section of the car.

"Well, thank you, young man. Very kind of you." Bill pulled out some cash from his money clip in his pocket and handed it over as Nana bent and crawled inside, followed by Lisa.

"Certainly, sir. Your grandson is a favorite here at the Renaissance Grand. We'll always do what we can to take care of him—and his family."

The bench seat was a soft, taupe leather and it curved around the inside of the stretched middle of the car like a snake waking up from a nap. Overhead, blue lights twinkled in a matching taupe fabric sky. Opposite the seating was an extended mirrored bar, stocked with shining crystal and a row of high-end bottles.

Once Bill slid onto the seat, the door closed with a satisfying sound. The partition between all the opulence and the driver's area lowered and a man in a black jacket turned to face his passengers.

"Is everything to your satisfaction?"

Nana spoke up. "Oh yes. It's beautiful back here. I feel like a movie star."

Her eyes twinkled a bit, like the little lights in the ceiling, as she studied her surroundings.

"Wonderful, ma'am. My name is Brent. I'll be your driver today for your trip to Lake Mead and back. Should you need anything, please press the red button on the edge of the partition." He pointed to a light in the corner. "Otherwise, please enjoy your ride with Limovegas."

Several minutes passed and they hadn't moved. Bill and Nana were scrolling through the lists for the onboard entertainment system and settled on a station that played big band standards from the 1940s.

"Remind you of anything, dear?" Bill looked at Nana with kind eyes.

It would have been so much easier for Lisa if he hadn't been such a sweet man. It was going to break his heart when she had to step in and call off the wedding. She didn't want to do that, but she still couldn't see a way around it. Tonight, after they'd had a memorable day in a beautiful setting, she'd have to sit them down and explain.

Maybe having one last day of memories together would help soften the blow.

She hoped so because it was becoming increasingly clear that the necessary words to come would be some of the hardest she'd ever spoken in her life.

The door to the limousine opened back up and sunshine streamed in.

Ryan climbed in. Lisa couldn't contain her confusion. "Your break just ended. You should be playing now, right?"

He slid to the edge of the bench seat. "I quit."

"I know. You announced it last night. This is your last tournament. So why aren't you in it?"

"No, I quit early. I cashed in my chips. I didn't want to leave you here with Pops and Gina Mae by yourself." He looked at his grandfather. "You told me to go out with a bang, Pops."

Bill pointed a mockingly-stern finger at Ryan. "So I did. But I didn't tell you to be a quitter, son."

"I'd already made my decision. It was just time."

Ryan took the cap off a bottle and poured a little bit of amber liquid over two cubes of ice. "Not as good as last night's, but it'll do. Pops, you want one?"

His grandfather smiled with a gleam in his eye and then looked at Nana. "Don't mind if I do indulge my inner Irishman a bit. Would you like anything, dear?"

As her grandmother nodded politely, Lisa couldn't help but frown a bit. Nana never drank, but she'd had champagne last night, and now she was studying the sleek bar inside the limo. Lisa smoothed away a non-existent speck of fuzz on the dark blue denim covering her legs as she thought. She was no teetotaler, but it would be harder to evaluate Nana's true condition if she had a glass of anything right now.

"Lisa?" Ryan tapped her on the shoulder and she felt a small spark, stronger than static electricity, where his finger touched the lightweight, crochet-style sweater. "How about you?"

"No thanks." Lisa felt totally drained—by the travel, by the situation with Nana, by what she knew was to come, and by her increasing awareness of Ryan's smooth presence.

This morning, as she got dressed and tried to sort out her thoughts about the evening before—especially how it ended—she knew she'd see Ryan again, but she'd been thankful for the buffer that his tournament and this day trip would provide. The hours at the lake were supposed to give her time to think through what she needed to say to Nana and Bill, build her courage, and let her do what had to be done without thinking about how just for one small moment she'd felt secure in Ryan's arms, like a promise that everything would be taken care of somehow.

Now that he was here, sitting next to her, Lisa felt completely insecure.

Like she didn't know where to start.

She knew where she had to go. Back home to Texas with Nana, and only Nana. But she didn't know how to get there.

"How about this, then?" Ryan handed her a bottle of sparkling water and twisted off the cap.

"That'll work great, thank you." Lisa held the bottle out slightly. "Nana? How about one of these?"

"Yes, please, Lisa Marie."

Ryan reached for another bottle, opened it, and then looked point-blank at Lisa before handing the water to Nana. "Lisa Marie?"

She shrugged. "My mama liked Elvis."

"You're in the right town."

"So it seems. At least she didn't name me Peanut Butter and Banana, right?"

"Or Hound Dog."

"That would have been tough in junior high." Lisa couldn't help but laugh a little as she answered.

"You might have gotten in a fight over it and had to spend the night doing some jailhouse rock."

Oh no. He wasn't going there, was he? "As long as some blue suede shoes came with my prison jumpsuit, I probably wouldn't have minded. I had a thing for shoes back then. Still do, actually."

Lisa wiggled her toes, where they stuck out of the little hole at the tip of her favorite casual wedges.

"I see that. You had some nice ones on last night. You picked a great outfit on short notice."

"Thanks." Lisa took a long sip from the curvy green bottle. "You paid for a great outfit on short notice."

Ryan pressed his lips together. It gave his face an almost stern air. "Lisa, you don't owe me anything. You and I are kind of in this boat together."

"Kind of?" She shifted in her seat, turning her back slightly on the older couple at the far end of the bench. Bill was pointing out landmarks and scenery to Nana as they drove by with Glenn Miller tunes filling the car with punctuating brass.

Ryan leaned back against the soft, stuffed leather. "I've been doing some thinking."

Me too, Lisa thought.

But...she was pretty sure Ryan wasn't talking about that. He'd probably kissed a thousand girls in his tenure as a Las Vegas card shark. Last night couldn't possibly have registered on his radar the way it registered on her slightly-less-experienced one.

So, she settled on a reply that was slightly more casual. "Oh?"

"I know we both think we need to stop tomorrow's ceremony from happening. But what if we can't?"

Lisa tucked her water bottle into a nearby cupholder. "Well, that's not an option. I have to get Nana to the doctor for tests. I'm just not comfortable with her making a life change like marriage until I know one way or another. I don't think she fully understands what she's consenting to. Have you heard anything from either one of them on where they're going to live? How they'll manage money and retirement funds—not that Nana has many, but they're still hers. Have you heard any plans for anything other than tomorrow? They sound like a couple of crazy teenagers headed for a drive-through chapel. I can't have Nana wake up the next day and realize she's made a terrible mistake. Not on my watch."

Ryan stole a glance back at his grandfather, then looked back at Lisa. "No, I haven't. But I also know this is the happiest I've seen Pops in I don't know how long. Something about seeing Gina Mae again has brought back some long-lost meaning to his life."

"Ryan. You told me we were in this together. You told me you were going to help me end this. Don't get sentimental on me."

"I am. I've just seen a lot of guys make big mistakes that have cost them everything they've worked for. I don't want to see you do the same. What happens when Gina Mae decides to never speak to you again because all she can see is that you're standing in the way of her happiness? She's an adult. You don't even have a diagnosis from a doctor, much less the necessary paperwork to put you in charge of the decisions in her life."

Lisa lowered her head into her cupped hands. He was right.

She'd always known the conversation would be tough, but she'd assumed if she could just find the right words, she could get Nana to understand. But even though they'd been a team for decades and relied on each other's steady counsel, what if Nana stopped listening now? What then?

Ryan placed a hand on her back. He didn't pat or rub, just laid it there—a silent acknowledgment of the fact that there were no easy answers. There weren't easy answers for this situation with Nana, and there weren't any easy answers for why she'd kissed this man last night and liked it. Or why just the simple touch of his hand over her spine made her feel protected.

"Why don't you just try and enjoy the day, Lisa? We'll think of something together."

Together.

Ryan's hand remained softly in place. He didn't let go. And somehow, that made Lisa feel a little less daunted by everything she knew was to come.

"Can I ask you something?" Ryan spoke with a slightly lower volume, but not exactly a whisper.

"Sure. I guess so. What?" She tried to brush off the uneasy quiver in her stomach that twitched as she tried to figure out what Ryan was getting at.

"They're not listening—they're back in the 1940s with their Glenn Miller." Ryan nodded toward Bill and Nana. "So I need you to be totally honest with me, Lisa. If your Nana marries my Pops tomorrow, what's the worst that could happen? What couldn't be fixed? Do you see the looks on their faces? Don't you think they deserve the happiness being back together brings each other?"

Lisa opened her mouth to reply. Then shut it firmly closed, trying to shove back the tears that just popped up without warning. She couldn't look at Ryan.

She certainly couldn't look at Nana and Pops.

What couldn't be fixed? Her heart, for starters. She'd be alone. Nana needed her, but if Lisa was truly honest, she needed Nana just as much. Maybe more. Nana was the living scrapbook to her childhood. If she wanted to know anything about her life as a child, she'd ask Nana. Even if she ever saw her mother again, Lisa doubted that the woman would remember anything. Her mother's unconditional love ended the minute she filled a glass or sat down to get a hit.

Pamela Fleming was a directionless mess.

Just like Lisa would be without Nana.

But even though Ryan had asked for Lisa's honesty, she couldn't tell him these deep fears. It just sounded so selfish.

"She has to get evaluated by a doctor. I need to know if her behavior lately is part of normal aging—or if it's something more."

"Lisa, there are doctors in Las Vegas. Beyond the Strip, this is a very normal town. Good people who work hard to provide for their families live here. There are suburbs. Shopping centers. There are Walmarts, for Heaven's sake. It doesn't look much different than Texas, I'd wager. Couldn't she see a doctor here?"

"I'm sure there are doctors here, Ryan, but how can I manage that from Port Provident? I have one week off for Spring Break, but then I'm due back in a classroom until the end of May. I have a contract. I don't get the luxury of just walking off from a table when I've had enough."

She knew that blow was a little low, but she shrugged it off. Sometimes the truth hurt.

Just like Ryan's probing question a few seconds ago.

"I walked off because it didn't matter anymore. My family did. My Pops did. The woman he wants to marry did. I didn't need to bring home another pot. I already knew it, but you helped me see it. I'm just trying to help you see it from their perspective, too."

"But Ryan, you and I talked about this. Where would they live?"

"At Pops' assisted living facility," Ryan said it with total clarity, like it was the obvious solution.

"You said last night that your big jackpots brought you the ability to pay for a place that's the best in this part of the country. Need I remind you that there's no teaching jackpot? I can't afford to pay Nana's bill there, and neither can Nana. And the district is talking about budget cuts next year. That always makes me nervous."

He picked his drink up from the cupholder and took a quick swallow. "So what if I just kept paying for it?"

Lisa cocked her head. "Listen to yourself. Yesterday, you were convinced I was a gold digger using my great-grandmother to come after your money. Today, you're offering to pay her housing bills for the rest of her life? You don't make any sense, Ryan McBride."

"I'm not trying to make sense. I'm trying to make my Pops happy. I've just realized I am willing to take a loss if that means he wins. What about you, Lisa?"

"I'm not much of a gambler, Ryan."

"Don't you love the theatre?"

She didn't see how the two had any connection. "Yes, obviously. But what does that have to do with anything?"

"Happily Ever After. Don't you believe in that?"

"Of course I do, Ryan."

Well, except when it came to her real life.

A real, mother-daughter relationship? *Happily Never After.*

The Broadway role she'd earned but couldn't have because she'd refused to put her morals to the side of the casting couch, as one director insisted? *Happily Never After.*

The fiancé who had dumped her two years ago because he "wanted more"—which was shorthand for the realization that his champagne tastes and social mobility needs were never going to get met by being paired with a drama teacher? *Happily Never After.*

"But those are all stories. Notice that they don't keep going after everyone gets their feel-good ending. The curtain goes down. But once Nana says 'I do,' her story keeps going. And I'm responsible for it."

"Lisa, your Nana is in her eighties?" He looked at her, head slightly askance.

"In her nineties."

He nodded. "Exactly. And she's probably made a mistake or two, right?"

"Well, sure." Where was he going with this?

"But more often than not, hasn't she gotten it right?" Ryan smiled casually. "She raised you. Pops raised me. I'd guess neither of them guessed they'd be raising their kids' kids. They probably wondered where they'd gone wrong with their own kids and were afraid of how everything was going to work out. But I think I turned out okay. And from what I see of you, I'm pretty sure you did too."

Ryan reached out and took Lisa's hand and squeezed lightly.

She couldn't help but nod. His words made a lot of sense.

"So, if I go along with this, and something goes wrong, what do I do?" She started to move her hand from under the protective cover of Ryan's, then hesitated.

"Break out into a song and start some coordinated dancing in the middle of the street. Isn't that what all of you theatre people do?" His smile inched out just a little further, showing straight white teeth that caught her gaze and held tight.

"Sometimes." She wiggled her fingers a bit, threading them through Ryan's. Somehow, even though she hadn't known him long, she already felt like she knew him well. And she knew he meant it. He wouldn't leave her to face this alone. "So you'll be in my flash mob?"

"Always, babe. Let's just have a fun day with the people we love and let the cards fall where they may."

AFTER A SIGHTSEEING trip at the Hoover Dam, Pops and Gina Mae scooted out as soon as the limo stopped in front of the landing which led to Lake Mead Dinner Cruise.

"Dinner on the water? Oh, how lovely." Gina Mae couldn't contain her excitement. "Bill, did you plan this?"

"No, I told Ryan I wanted to do something special for you today, but he put everything together."

Ryan closed the door to the limo after everyone had exited. "Well, I had some ideas. Winter at the concierge desk did all the scheduling this morning after I headed to the tournament."

"Still. You're a very thoughtful young man, Ryan. Thank you for taking the time to make today special. And thank you for coming with us. I thought you were going to be working," Gina Mae said.

"Well, I did too, Gina Mae. But you know, things change."

She patted her silver curls as a small gust of dry wind picked up around them. "I certainly do. Who would have ever guessed I'd find Bill again. And on a computer web site place. Things have certainly changed from our day. But I'm glad they have."

Pops and Nana held hands, walking at a pace dictated by their age, but with footsteps in sync. Pops held the door at the dock for Gina Mae, and she thanked him with a smile. The years fell away as her eyes caught his and Ryan couldn't help but see the girl she must have been before World War II arrived and tore her away from his grandfather.

Ryan stopped near the sidewalk and turned slightly, waiting for Lisa. He held the door open for her, wondering if he'd get a smile like Pops had received.

Had he really just called her "babe" in the limo? He certainly hadn't planned it. And the more he thought about it, the more he felt like he'd just spiraled into some alternate world of Vegas cheesiness. Except that wasn't how he wanted Lisa to think of him at all. They were in this situation together, and if he was honest with himself, her opinion now mattered to him.

Lisa looked up, a honey-gold sparkle in her eyes. The fears and worries that had been so evident earlier had been washed away. She looked beautiful, in a simple way that he hadn't often seen in his years of living under the bright lights on the Strip.

Last night, he'd definitely taken notice of her—even though he'd initially tried not to. He'd wanted to treat her like an opponent, come up with a strategy to clean out her chips and send her packing.

But then he had a chance to talk to her, to get to know the real Lisa. And somehow, in that one evening, she'd been able to solidify his resolve to leave gaming and to find a way to start fresh and pursue his restless desire to do something with meaning.

She couldn't possibly know what those few hours and her listening ear had done for him.

Once they were inside and their tickets had been checked, Lisa walked over to some of the photos on the wall and studied the visual history of the Hoover Dam and Lake Mead. Ryan stopped beside her.

"It's all going to work out, you know that, right?"

"For whom?"

He pointed his thumb at the couple on the other side of the small room. "Well, them. But I think it'll work out for us too."

She turned away from the pictures and looked at him.

"I mean, I think we'll be okay because they'll be okay." First, he was calling her "babe" and now he was calling them an "us"?

Rookie mistakes, all of them.

He wasn't even half a day removed from his days as a professional gambler and he was tripping all over himself like he hadn't done in a decade.

Not smooth at all, McBride.

Besides, it wasn't like he was looking for someone.

She smiled up at him, clearly picking up on his mistake. The peaches-and-cream vibe she gave off, from the array of dark gold in her curls, to her ivory complexion, to her honey eyes, to those soft lips and the slightly askew crocheted sweater that revealed the tank top that contained all her curves—it was distracting him in a way that none of his professional training had prepared him for.

So, maybe he *wasn't* exactly looking for someone.

But maybe he'd found something he hadn't been looking for.

He wasn't a professional anymore. But he knew some of those lessons would stay with him for the rest of his life. They'd become a part of his personality, they made up who he was. And the number one lesson of playing poker is finding a way to win with the hand you were dealt.

Ryan's thoughts continued to spin as they boarded the paddle wheeler. Sunset was on the way and he could feel the change in the air. Tonight, it seemed to signal more than just a natural course of the day. It felt like a sign.

When he'd sat at the table, he'd always tried to read the signs around him. He'd been dealt a crazy hand of grandfather-planned-surprise-wedding-to-his-teenage-girlfriend. But he wondered if he could turn it into a winner for everyone involved.

"Tell me something," Lisa said as she stopped at the rail near the front of the boat. Her hands rested on the red-painted wood that bordered the white gingerbread beneath. "How'd you get the nickname Lucky Charm? Even the manager in the boutique called you that instead of Ryan."

"Most people do. It comes from my last name, McBride. It's Irish, obviously, so when I started winning tournaments out of nowhere, some commentators said I must have the luck of the Irish. It evolved into Lucky Charm, and then it kind of stuck."

"I don't think I've ever really had a nickname." She watched the waves lap around the edge of the boat as the paddle wheel began to push them out across the lake.

The night breeze picked her curls up and tossed them around her face and shoulders, like confetti in a parade.

"Do you want me to give you one?" Ryan leaned one arm on the rail next to her and turned to face her. The last red rays of the sun gleamed behind her profile, lining her features with a burnished glow.

Ryan knew he'd seen a lot of things over the years. Some good, some bad. Some incredible. But this was a moment he knew he wanted to hold onto for a lifetime. A gentle breeze, a striking sunset, and a quietly beautiful woman who'd captured the corners of an imagination he'd long thought was in hibernation—or worse.

A wry smile feathered her lips. "I think I'm too old for that now. I'm just Lisa."

"No, you're not."

She turned toward him, shifting the setting sun's light to frame her hair. "Come on. I'm just a theatre geek. We don't have teams or secret handshakes or anything like that."

"Well, we're kind of on the same team now." Ryan pointed back toward the dining area, where he knew Pops and Gina Mae had gone to sit down.

"But no secret handshake."

Instinct took over, sending a little pang of fear through Ryan. He never acted on instinct. He acted on the odds which were most likely to result in victory.

But with victory came surrender of the other side, and he'd never wanted anything more than the surrender of Lisa in his arms. And the odds said the most likely way to get there was to let his instinct run wild.

"No secret handshake. Just this."

His instinct ran straight to Lisa's mouth and the overwhelming need he had to taste her and touch that edge of light and shadow on her skin.

Ryan leaned down as swiftly as the breeze that swirled around them. As he got the contact he craved, the slight intake of breath Lisa made caused him to pause.

The adrenaline screeched to a halt in his veins, like a dam struggling to hold back a freak unexpected rainstorm.

Lisa lifted her arms and laid them over his shoulders, and the flood of his heightened awareness of her and only her crested the top of the dam and broke free. He kissed her hard, and as she slid tentative fingertips through the edge of his hair on his neck, he pulled forward and kissed her deeply.

It felt like the Fourth of July instead of the day before St. Patrick's Day. Lisa pulled a little closer to Ryan and sparks of fireworks lit in every space and hollow where their bodies touched and the thick yarn of her light sweater pressed tightly between them.

He wasn't calculating odds, counting cards, or looking for signs. Ryan's eyes were closed and his mind was processing only the feel of her in his arms and the hasty sound of her breathing just below his ear.

The ringing of a loud brass bell nearby crashed through the moment with the sharp finality of watching an opponent rake your pile of chips into his own. There was nothing you could do except know the moment was gone.

But Ryan knew this moment would be with him in his mind for a long time to come.

Lisa stood rooted to the deck, not following the crowd inside for dinner.

"You're not playing me, right, Ryan?" She looked at him, then back out toward the water, where what was left of the sun was now nothing more than a dusky haze atop the surface.

Her words stung, like a razor blade that just barely misses the prescribed angle while shaving.

"That wasn't a game, Lisa."

"So do you know what we're doing here?" Her eyes seemed to plead with him for an answer.

"I think I'm spending the evening with a beautiful woman because I enjoyed her company a great deal last night." He couldn't decide if it was a good idea to reveal that or not. As the words came out of his mouth, he felt a little exposed, and he wasn't used to that.

But he could see that the full truth mattered to Lisa. And if the full truth was too much, she'd be on a plane in a few days, anyway.

Unless...

The thought parked in Ryan's head before he could fully form it.

He looked at Lisa, now dusted with the shadows of the oncoming evening instead of the copper sunset that had just highlighted her only a few minutes ago. The sun seemed to have set quickly tonight. Even more quickly, it seemed that their relationship had changed.

Ryan hoped it was changing for the better.

He forced himself to complete the half-thought in his mind. He hoped it was changing for the better because he didn't want Lisa to get on a plane in a few days. He wanted her to stay here, to get to know her better, and to see if his hunch that there was something between them that went beyond the situation they'd been thrust into by their love-struck grandparents.

"Ryan, you don't have to say that just because we're forced together in a slightly crazy situation."

"I'm not. Do you not believe I'd want to spend time with you?"

Her brow furrowed as she tried to place her words. "I think you're the Lucky Charm of Las Vegas. Everyone knows you and everyone seems to want a piece of you. I don't quite understand what a teacher from Texas would bring to the table to compete with your everyday world."

"Maybe I'm tired of my everyday world. Maybe I want something different." Ryan paused for a second and stared out at the same small dips and swells of the water that Lisa was focused on. "Maybe there's no maybe about it."

"I know you said that you were tired of being on the poker tour and you wanted to do something with more meaning. But Ryan, don't you think making too many changes at once is a little dangerous?"

"I've spent the last ten years on the edge. Every time I sat down at a table, Lisa, I could lose everything at the turn of a card. What's dangerous for most people *is* everyday life for me."

He wished she'd look at him, but she kept her eyes steady on the lake. "Can you promise me this isn't some elaborate bluff?"

"My bluffing days are over, sweetheart," he said solemnly.

Lisa turned and faced him. "I want to believe you."

"Lisa, your stories last night helped me see that I'd made the right decision. There's more for me out there, and you helped me know that when I questioned the announcement I'd made. Your concern for your grandmother made me really stop and think through this situation with Pops and it led me to the conclusion that I have to support him in the decisions he makes for his life, not expect him to conform to what's convenient for mine. You gave me a clarity I couldn't find on my own for not one, but two, major decisions I needed to make in my life."

Ryan reached out his hand and gently cupped it around Lisa's forearm. At his touch, she pulled her gaze up and turned her head toward him.

He decided to lay it all out there. If she turned him down, at least he'd know and he could get used to the idea that she'd be leaving soon on a plane. At least he'd know and he could pick up the uncertainty of his new-found retirement and go from there.

"It's a beautiful night and I'm here on this boat with a beautiful woman. I can't let Pops have all the fun. I'd like to take the other Fleming on a date right now. Would you please be my date tonight?"

Lisa swallowed and Ryan watched the set of her jaw and the contraction of her slender throat. He felt a chunk of ice slide to the pit of his stomach. Clearly, she wasn't interested.

He couldn't blame her for still wanting to focus solely on what was right for her Nana.

"I suppose I can trust you. Those two chaperones wouldn't let you try anything out of line."

Ryan shook his head and the ice melted with the warm relief that kicked in his veins.

"No. I only bring the finest chaperones out to impress the ladies. I require an average vintage of ninety years."

Lisa smiled, and Ryan knew he could look at her face like this all night.

NANA AND BILL HAD BEEN feted with a table for two near the dance floor. The cozy round table had been set with special china and crystal. The candlelight reflected off the facets of the crystal and glowed on the glaze of the china, making the setup look fit for a fairy tale.

The crew had reserved a table near the window for Lisa and Ryan. Lisa had hoped to sit with Nana and Bill, but to see the looks on their faces as people stopped by their table and congratulated them warmed her heart over and over and over again.

"They look so happy, don't they?" Lisa spoke out loud, but the words were almost as much for her as for Ryan.

"You could be too, you know." Ryan poured a glass of wine from the bottle the server sat at the edge of the table. The red liquid swirled around in the glass and rippled gently with the rocking of the paddle wheeler as it chugged on its journey across Lake Mead.

Lisa tried to keep the sigh inside.

"I heard that." Ryan took a thoughtful sip of his wine. "Why do you disagree?"

"I don't know."

The waiter brought a narrow silver tray lined with a blue napkin and tucked full of crusty sourdough rolls. Ryan took a roll, placed it on a small white plate, and handed it to Lisa.

"I think you do. Look, Lisa, I don't expect you to marry me tonight, but we're in this together for the long haul. You are the primary caregiver for your great-grandmother. I'm the primary caregiver for my grandfather. They're getting married." He pulled apart his roll and swiped creamy butter on the exposed fluffy bread. "We're in this for the long haul at one level or another, you know? You can be honest with me. I promise."

It was nothing more than a reflex, a long-conditioned reaction to keep from being hurt, but Lisa shook her head mildly.

"You can't?" Ryan's tone of voice held a hint of surprise.

Lisa thought about what her body language had just conveyed. "It's been a long time, Ryan."

"Since what? A date?" He leaned slightly forward in his chair.

"That too."

"And?" He wouldn't give up. He was reading her as clearly as if she wore a neon Vegas sign.

"Trusted."

"Trusted. So you don't think you can trust me?"

Lisa stabbed at squares of lettuce with her fork, trying to collect her thoughts under the guise of eating. "It's not that."

"It's something. Look, Lisa, you're a good actress, but you're not that good. Changes are coming for each of us in our families. But I can't help you—and you can't help me—if you're not honest with me."

She swirled the cabernet in her glass and then took a long sip of liquid courage. "I just don't trust too many people. I don't have a reason to."

"Nana's not a reason?" He was making this hard and it was making her mad. She didn't want to have this conversation. She didn't want to open up to Ryan McBride. She wanted to look at his eyes, pretend as if for a few daysthat someone in her life didn't have an ulterior motive, then get Nana back home to Dr. Reynolds.

And then take care of herself.

Alone.

Without worrying anyone, especially Nana.

Or herself, if she was extending this honesty thing all the way.

"Nana's the best reason. But I don't even know you, Ryan."

He smiled, teeth sharkishly grinning in the midst of the dusting of beard across his chin and cheeks. "So what do you want to know? We've already discussed my nickname. And we never need to go there again. If I never get called Lucky Charm again, that's a good thing."

Lisa took the opportunity to turn the spotlight off her. "Why? It's kind of cool that people know you and they like you."

"Well, it's cool if you're a multicolored marshmallow or a leprechaun on a cereal box. Not if you're a thirty-three-year-old man. Ladies aren't generally impressed by leprechauns."

"The lady in the boutique said you used to date some European supermodel. So I guess someone was impressed."

"She was a poker player, not a supermodel. And it was all part of the game."

The waiter removed the salad plates and replaced them with a plate artfully styled with a small steak, several grilled shrimp, garlic mashed potatoes, and some roasted carrots shining with a light honey glaze. Lisa silently prayed that drool didn't begin to snake down her chin.

"The game? Isn't it funny how everyone's playing a game?" She took a bite of candied carrot, letting the sweet taste overpower some of the savory conversation.

"Are you?" Ryan polished off the grilled shrimp in quick succession between the beats of conversation. "I've played all sorts of games for a long time. Games at the table, games of popularity. All that business. I'm looking forward to just being me for a while."

Lisa still didn't know how to give Ryan the answer he was looking for.

She didn't even know how to give herself the answer.

"Who is that?"

Ryan didn't waste any time taking a bite out of the filet mignon. "A guy who lived the dream and then woke up. Who are you, Lisa Marie?"

"A girl who tried to live the dream, but it turned into a nightmare."

She clamped her mouth shut. She'd said too much and the fear of the honesty gave her a paralyzing case of conversational lockjaw.

Ryan didn't reply and Lisa decided to keep looking down and focus on what she could control.

Carrots and mashed potatoes.

It was a sad commentary, she realized. A good-looking man who had been considerate to her wanted to get to know her better, and all she could do was stare down carbohydrates.

"I don't want to pretend anymore," she said softly, chasing a carrot around her plate with the fork. "I don't want to be an actress. I just want to be me."

"So I'll ask again. Who is that, Lisa Marie Fleming?" Ryan's voice was soft but insistent.

Lisa looked up. She knew the expression on her face was blank, like the laundered white tablecloth covering their table. It embarrassed her to have nothing to give.

She felt the flush in her cheeks and the sweat just under the skin of her fingertips.

Ryan stood up from his chair and came over next to Lisa.

She opened her mouth to speak. Ryan pressed a strong finger against her lips. She could taste the faint hint of butter and honey.

"*Sssh*." He kept the finger in place. He lowered it, trailing the edge over the curve of her lip and tapping her chin once. "Why don't we just not talk?"

Ryan held out his hand and kept a steady gaze on Lisa until he got what he wanted.

The sticky feeling in the swirls and grooves of her fingertips came alive like microscopic lines of cinders the instant she put her hand in Ryan's. The contours of his hand cradled hers and he tugged gently as she scooted her chair back and took a small step.

A silver-haired woman in a blue lamé-trimmed pantsuit stood behind a small glittery DJ booth. She tapped the microphone for attention twice. "We're going to get the dance portion of our dinner cruise started with the traditional Anne Murray. This one is for all the lovebirds on board."

"We can't pass up the traditional Anne Murray. Just come with me, Lisa. You don't have to say anything. I promise."

As the familiar sounds of the Canadian singer's most famous hit began to fill all the corners of the paddle wheeler, Lisa let Ryan lead her to the parquet dance floor. Purple and blue spotlights flicked back and forth, casting a violet tint on Ryan's arm as he wrapped it comfortably around her waist.

"Could I at least have this dance for tonight, Lisa?" Ryan asked, echoing the theme of Anne Murray's words.

Lisa nodded and felt a shy smile on her lips. Ryan's arms felt solid, strong. Just like they'd felt on the deck earlier when he'd pulled her in for that kiss.

Maybe it was the kiss that had gotten her so tongue-tied. She wasn't usually like this. She was trained to speak to people. It frustrated her that she couldn't speak to Ryan, that she couldn't just carry on a conversation and answer his questions.

A mirror ball the size of a basketball twirled just above them, throwing more sparkle and light on the dance floor. Three other couples staked their place and tapped and twirled along with the music.

Lisa left all her dance training by the wayside and just swayed in Ryan's arms.

She wanted to just be.

Who was Lisa Marie Fleming? At this moment, she knew the precise answer.

She was a girl who just wanted to be supported for who she was. She wanted someone to stand beside her and be there for the future. She wanted to dream and inspire and have someone understand why. She wanted someone who would 'get' her, with no reservations, now that Nana was exiting stage right from her day-to-day life.

"I'm scared, Ryan." Lisa's whisper held up just barely over the start of a Frank Sinatra standard.

Ryan looked down, locked his gaze on hers, and pulled her a little tighter as she rocked back and forth like a metronome, doing the same movement over and over because it didn't require any more thought.

"The only person who really knows me is Nana. Who am I when she's gone?"

Ryan brushed back a lock of Lisa's hair.

"The woman she raised you to be. Her legacy."

A tear slipped from the corner of Lisa's eye. It ran down the valley beside her nose. Ryan brushed it away with the care of collecting a rare diamond.

"She's the only person who hasn't pulled the rug out from under me. My mother left because I cut into her personal life. My Broadway dreams were done when I realized the people who didn't expect me to sacrifice my morals were few and far between. The man who said he loved me didn't love me enough to let me work through some changes in my life."

"Do you feel this, Lisa?" Ryan flexed the muscles in the arm around her waist.

She nodded.

"It's not going anywhere. You have a friend for life. No matter where life takes you, I'm not walking the other way."

Lisa gave a very unladylike sniff as she tried to choke back another tear. "But why not? You barely know me."

"Maybe. But I know my Pops. And if your Nana was special enough to stay in his mind through more than sixty years of living, then I think I'd be crazy to assume her great-granddaughter didn't have some of those same qualities."

Squares of light from overhead dappled Ryan's face, highlighting his eyes. The violet of the lights somehow made his eyes an even deeper blue. Lisa felt herself being pulled into them, like a rip current off a rolling seashore.

"I'd call it placing an educated bet. I'm taking the knowledge of what I see before me, calculating the odds, and then committing to the play."

His words made total sense to Lisa. She picked up her feet and started to shuffle a little across their corner of the dance floor. Ryan matched her steps one by one until they were both in time with the music—and with each other.

Six decades after last seeing Bill McBride, this week's reunion with the man brought a genuine twinkle to Nana's face. Ryan was right—there was something between the two grandparents, a lesson she could learn if she chose to be the pupil instead of the teacher for just a moment.

It was more than something you'd see in a TV movie, more genuine than anything that could be memorized from a script and brought to life.

It *was* life. Real life. And Lisa didn't want to live in the shadows of the past, haunted by the questions of decisions made long ago.

On this crazy makeshift dance floor in the middle of a replica paddle wheel boat, with the sounds of classic crooners filling the air, there were only bright spotlights, live colors, dancing diamonds of light. There were no shadows.

Lisa longed to come out of the shadows which had started haunting her as a little girl, when her mother stopped coming back to Nana's house. She tugged Ryan toward the center of the dance floor, where the colors glowed the most strongly, and she spoke in a language she knew he'd understand.

"I'm all in."

NANA BRUSHED PAST BY Lisa, held tightly in Bill's arms. He reached up and out and twirled Nana with practiced ease. Lisa smiled just watching her. She looked sure-footed and at-ease, as though she was still that girl caught up in a summer romance before enemies dropped bombs and pointed guns half a world away.

On their next round of the dance floor, Bill and Nana slowed alongside Lisa and Ryan. "You two look like you're enjoying yourselves. Bill, isn't it like we're looking in some kind of mirror? That's just what we looked like almost eighty years ago."

Bill nodded in hearty agreement. "She looks just like you, the night that I took you to the dance at the Mueller family's barn. You wore that white dress with the yellow flowers embroidered on it. I never forgot how beautiful you looked that night. And it does seem that Lisa got a good dose of those genes. You're both beautiful—God knew what he was doing with you two."

He lifted Nana's hand and gave it a gentle kiss.

Lisa found herself caught up in something about the boat ride, the classic dance standards coming through the speakers, and this sweet man whose love for her grandmother had stretched across more than three-quarters of a century.

She looked up at Ryan and saw the same eyes as the smitten older man next to them—only, a few shades darker, and not surrounded by the lines of life. She'd heard it said so many times that "character is who you are when no one is looking." Bill McBride's character was evident in every loving gesture, every compliment, every sentence he spoke. He loved Gina Mae Fleming. He loved his grandson.

Ever the dreamer, Lisa had always hoped for a love like that. And she'd always gotten burned. But what if Bill McBride's love and decency were just as much of a genetic legacy as the shape of his Irish blue eyes?

Lisa knew what she wanted half a century from now. She wanted the chivalry, the caresses, the shared jokes that still made each other laugh. She wanted a lifetime love.

"What do you think He was doing with us, Pops?" Ryan chuckled and elbowed his grandfather playfully.

"Us? Well, my boy, we live in the luckiest town on earth. It only makes sense that he made us lucky in love." With anyone else, a bold statement like that would have been cloaked in mirth and said with a chuckle.

But with Bill, it came out as a statement of fact.

He believed it.

And as another song came on and Ryan pulled her close for a slow dance, Lisa believed it too.

She was falling for Ryan McBride. She didn't know how and she didn't know why, but she saw the starry skies out the back window of the boat, closed her eyes, and made a silent wish that the luck of the Irish would rub off on her heart too.

"I'm so glad you and Lisa decided to get married too." Nana used enough volume that no one could mistake what she'd said.

Lisa tugged a little on Ryan's sleeve, trying to encourage him back to dancing. Ryan looked at her, that heart-stopping blue barely visible between the squint of his eyelids.

"What is she talking about?"

"I told you. She needs to go to Dr. Reynolds soon." Lisa racked her brain, trying to think of a way to change the subject.

She didn't want her luck to run out before it ever started.

On their way back to Las Vegas, Nana and Pops dozed in a corner of the limousine's long, curved seat.

"They've had a big day. And a bigger one ahead tomorrow."

"*Mmm-hmm*." Lisa tried unsuccessfully to stifle a yawn. "I'm sorry, it's not the company, I swear."

"I know it's not. I'm used to late nights. I doubt you are. High school theatre is probably over by ten."

She laughed as she nodded. "Something like that. The kids may not be through, but they can take it to the local pancake place. Their teacher sure is finished. I'm like Cinderella's carriage. I turn into a pumpkin at midnight."

"I bet you're the prettiest gourd out there."

"You sure know how to compliment a girl, Mr. High Roller."

Ryan leaned back in the seat. "Nah. My high-rolling days are over, remember?"

"I do. Have you thought anymore about what you want to do?" Lisa kicked off her shoes and tucked her legs and feet up on the seat, underneath her. The position pulled her dark wash jeans tight and showed off her assets in a way that began to drive Ryan more than a little crazy.

"Well, I guess your Nana thinks we're actually getting married."

Lisa's immediate tension at Gina Mae's proclamation earlier told Ryan she knew far more than she was letting on. But other activities on the remainder of the boat ride prevented him from probing further.

A nice, quiet limousine ride, on the other hand, seemed like the perfect time to ask—and actually get an answer.

Lisa squirmed a bit in her seat. If she kept moving like that, he might not care what answer she gave.

"She heard about your announcement. I told her it was all a misunderstanding."

Good news traveled fast.

Ryan thought back to that kiss under the stars, and later, the feel of Lisa in his arms as they danced on that small dance floor. He turned over the moments in his mind, dissecting the sounds and emotions and the thoughts he'd had all night.

"What if it wasn't?"

She sat up straight. "What if what wasn't what?"

"A misunderstanding."

Her lips pursed as her eyes narrowed. The blue glow of the custom overhead lighting fell on her, making her look like a curious Smurf.

Ryan wasn't sure he'd seen anything more beautiful. Saturday morning cartoons had never made him feel like this. The anxious waiting he'd felt during commercial breaks, waiting to get back to the animated action didn't come close to the swift acceleration of pulse and kick of adrenaline swishing through his veins as he anticipated Lisa's reply.

"Like you and me?"

"Isn't that how it happens in the scripts and stories? Boom, you just know? Like a Hallmark holiday movie—just at spring break, in Vegas?" He ran a hand through his hair. This wasn't going how he wanted it to.

Of course, he didn't know exactly how he wanted it to go.

He only knew that he wanted Lisa.

Wanted to know her better.

Wanted to ease the worry she seemed to carry with her like a well-worn handbag.

Wanted to kiss her deeply and find out what would make her wrap her arms around his neck again.

"But this is real life, not the theatre or the Hallmark Channel, Ryan. Who acts like that in real life?"

On one hand, Ryan knew she had a point. But on the other hand, he could think of evidence against real life.

"Them." He pointed back at the sleeping couple, Gina Mae's head tenderly resting on Pops' shoulder, their hands loosely clasped between them. "Me."

"You? No. You're Mr. Direct. The moment I met you, you tried cutting me down to size."

"I won't deny I wasn't happy to be there at the airport. But Lisa, the way I see it, you and I have a lot in common. In each of our own way, we're both dreamers. I'll risk everything for a good card. You'll slip into the world of a character. I'm a gambler by trade. I take risks. I've told you some of those moves are calculated. But you can't be a good gambler if you can't go with your gut. "

Ryan didn't want to hear her protest. He knew he was right. As she opened her mouth to speak, he leaned toward her and covered her mouth with his own.

Gently, at first, then instinct took over. He brushed his hands over her hair, feeling the soft curls and waves. He felt his fingers down the groove of her spine, first at her neck and then between her shoulder blades.

Ryan shifted his weight and moved his arms to frame Lisa's body. He braced his weight with his hands and waited for her to signal with a turn or a push that he'd gone too far by stealing another kiss tonight. He hesitated one moment, then one moment more, and then he was unable to hold back anymore.

The blood pounding in his ears drowned out any other soft sounds in the limo and the lingering light floral scent at the spot between Lisa's collarbones called to him like a magnet pulling in the direction of true north. He closed the kiss, lifted his head slightly, and moved his focus, nibbling along her jawline and caressing the slope of her neck. When he finally found the hollow he'd been searching for, he pressed a kiss in the soft curve and Lisa came alive with a low moan in her throat.

If the driver turned now and headed for the California coast, Ryan knew he still would not have enough time to kiss Lisa the way he wanted to.

She tangled searching fingers at the crown of his hair and Ryan almost lost all sense of himself at her own form of wordless risk-taking. Lightning storms were generally rare in the middle of the desert, but the electricity which flowed from Ryan to Lisa and back again drove him mad.

"See. I told you, Bill. You said that lady in the casino was wrong. I told you she said they were getting married." Gina Mae's voice held a small sound of sleepiness and a large dose of smug. "Won't a double wedding be fun, Bill? How lucky are we?"

Ryan decided there was no use trying to casually slide back to his portion of the bench seat. They'd been caught.

Lisa might have been worrying about a dementia diagnosis for her grandmother, but she clearly didn't need to concern herself with getting Nana checked for cataracts.

Caught. Red-handed.

And red-lipsticked. Ryan swiped a hand near his cheek, trying to wipe away some of the evidence. Then he stopped himself. No sense in denying it, really. They were two grown adults.

Plus, he'd enjoyed it. Really, really enjoyed it.

"Nana, remember what I told you earlier..." Lisa weighed in with some hesitation.

The older woman's clear eyes looked back blankly. "No, not really."

Lisa took a deep breath, then spoke with clear syllables and a deliberately slow cadence. "It was all a mistake. The reporter made a mistake."

"Well, really, she didn't," Ryan interjected himself casually into the conversation.

"Yes, she did."

He shook his head. "Nope. If we're going to discuss that interview, let's get it right."

"Ryan!"

He didn't know how she did it, but Lisa turned the four letters of his name into a whole different kind of four-letter word, just with her tone of voice.

"I told her I was retiring and then I threw in that I was getting married, just to mess with everyone." He raised his arms and locked his hands behind his head. "So she was just reporting what I told her."

"See, honey, the reporter wasn't lying." Nana just smiled.

"Nana! Don't you think I'd know if I was getting married?" Lisa looked at Gina Mae, then over to Ryan. The look on her face begged him for help.

But he hesitated. He *could* help Lisa, but not in the way that she was hoping for right this second.

Wouldn't that solve all her worries about taking care of Nana and paying for the expensive tests that were to come? She said she didn't want to accept his help in paying Nana's part of the assisted living facility expenses. But he also knew she likely hadn't come up with any way to make it happen on her own.

What if financial support from him wasn't a handout?

Even if it was just a temporary arrangement—the quickie annulment or divorce was just as common around Vegas as the quickie wedding—he could handle that. Just something to get Pops and Nana settled in their new place in a way that caused as few disruptions for them as possible.

And if Lisa chose to pay his investment back in another series of kisses like that last one, well, those would be acceptable terms.

"Don't you want to get married?" Ryan decided to put his plan in motion.

Her jaw popped open and her nostrils flared slightly with incredulity. "Aren't you supposed to be helping me?"

"You're not answering the question. I can't answer yours until you answer mine."

"Of course she does. She used to be engaged." Nana chimed in when Lisa wouldn't break the silence.

"Thank you, Gina Mae. Now we're getting somewhere." Ryan nodded, a gesture of thanks. "So, you used to be engaged. That means you're comfortable with the concept of marriage."

Lisa's jaw set like a steel trap closing in around prey. She refused to let any words escape.

The familiar tingle of adrenaline, of having an opponent on the run, began to percolate in Ryan's veins.

He wouldn't necessarily call Lisa an opponent.

But he didn't have any plans to stop until she called.

He'd come too far to fold now.

"So if it's not marriage, is it me?"

"I. Don't. Know. You." The syllables barely squeaked out.

"All evidence to the contrary. You're in the habit of kissing men you don't know, then?"

Pops cleared his throat. "Son, I think you're misunderstanding what she's saying. I don't know what you told that reporter, but I don't think you've ever been engaged before. At least not to my knowledge."

"Nope, Pops. This is a first for me."

"A first? It would have to have happened for it to be a first. Right now, it's still a zero. This is like trying to buy a burger with Monopoly money. Yeah, it looks kind of like money, but it doesn't spend in the real world."

"Lisa, your grandmother is asking for a double wedding. You're not going to give her what she wants for her special day?" He couldn't keep the grin off his face.

Now he was just having fun. He knew he'd have to ask her forgiveness later. He'd put some thought into it and come up with an appropriate plan.

It would probably involve kissing.

It would *definitely* involve kissing.

That is, if Lisa ever allowed him within fifty feet of her again.

The limo pulled up to the main doors of the Renaissance Grand. Their ride was over, but the discussion wasn't. He'd gone too far to back down now. Besides, Nana gave him a peck on the cheek as she exited the vehicle. At least one of the Fleming women wasn't offended.

Lisa looked at Ryan's outstretched hand, ready to assist her in exiting the limousine, then pushed past, giving herself a wide berth.

"I think when it comes to wedding gifts, normal people just ask for a blender," she said before walking through the sliding glass doors without so much as a backward look at her erstwhile fiancé.

Chapter Seven

LISA STUDIED THE PEDICURE menu as her toes splashed in the warm water in the foot box. Should she go with the cappuccino package or something soothing, like cucumber mint?

Definitely cucumber mint. She was still licking her wounds from last night.

And this pre-wedding spa time presented the last real opportunity for her to talk Nana out of walking down the aisle with Bill.

Maybe, Lisa thought, she needed a Valium pedicure. Cucumber might not be soothing enough to get her in the right frame of mind.

She still couldn't believe how Ryan turned on her in the limo last night. Yes, she'd agreed to move forward and not spoil Nana and Pops' happiness for the sake of all involved, but would it have killed the man to have told Nana the wedding rumor wasn't true?

Why wouldn't he have just told Nana no? Surely his plan of keeping everyone happy didn't extend to flat-out lying. Lisa couldn't go along with that.

"I think I want pineapple mango." Nana tapped the laminated plastic spa menu with her pointer finger. "What are you going to get, Lisa Marie?"

"I'm leaning toward cucumber mint."

"Oh, that sounds nice too. But I think I want something tropical," Nana said. "Should Bill and I go to Hawaii for our honeymoon? I've always wanted to go to Hawaii."

It was now or never.

"Nana, can I ask you something?"

Nana smiled, that same gentle look of grace and concern that had provided Lisa reassurance her entire life. Lisa tried to focus on that. And hoped against hope that she wouldn't wipe the smile off Nana's face with her words.

"Of course, Lisa Marie. What is it?"

The nail technicians came and sat at the foot of each pedicure chair and started the first part of the pedicure, mixing scented salts into the foot-sizes boxes of warm, bubbling water with the LED lights which alternated purple and blue.

Lisa sucked in a fortifying breath. "Do you really think you should be doing this?"

"I don't see why not. I don't think a pedicure will upset my blood pressure medication. Do you?"

"Not the pedicure, Nana. The wedding. Do you think you should be marrying Bill?"

There. She said it.

She wished she felt any kind of relief at getting that question off her chest, but instead. All she felt was cold dread as the seconds ticked by, waiting on Nana's answer.

"Of course. You don't?"

The technician clipped Nana's toenails, then began to scrub at her heels. Lisa's technician followed suit.

"Well, no. I don't."

The scraping motion kept brushing the most ticklish spot at the base of Lisa's arch. She began to giggle.

"Why are you laughing about it? What's so funny?"

"Feet, Nana." Lisa tried clenching her jaw—maybe that would hold the laugh inside as the technician continued to scrub a pumice stone over the tickle zone.

"You don't like Bill's feet, Lisa? What an odd reason."

Nana's nail technician moved easily to the right foot. Nana hadn't so much as flinched while the rough skin at the edge of her heel was polished off.

On the other hand, Lisa couldn't stop laughing. Acting like she was sitting in the front row at a comedy club was not helping the seriousness she needed to convey.

"Bill's feet are fine," Lisa spoke quickly as the technician switched to the other foot.

Nana swirled her feet back in the water. "Then what's the problem with him?"

"It's not him, Nana. It's you."

The look Nana gave Lisa could have started a lightning storm. Full of crackle and crash, her entire being showed that she didn't like the direction this conversation began to turn.

"My feet are fine, Lisa Marie," she said sternly. "And if you're trying to imply that other parts of me are not, then you are welcome to stay in the room this evening."

Finally, the pumice scrubbing torture ended. But Lisa was far from leaning back in the chair massager and relaxing. "Wait, what?"

"You heard me." Nana looked first to Lisa with a narrowed gaze. She then turned to the petite woman rubbing lotion on her feet. "Can you just skip everything and just polish my toes?"

The nail technician nodded, clearly keeping herself out of the conversation which kept increasing in heat every minute.

"You don't want me at your wedding, Nana?"

Nana pushed her shoulders back and sat up as tall as she could. "No."

Lisa never thought this would have been an easy conversation. She expected it to be difficult. She expected it to be direct.

She never expected Nana to cut her off.

"That'll do," Nana said to her nail technician. She swiveled out of the chair, away from Lisa, and slid her feet in a pair of orange disposable flip-flops. "Just charge this to my room, please. I need to leave."

"Nana, you do not need to leave. Please can we talk about this?" Lisa started to hop out of her chair, then realized she was covered from pinky toe to knee-joint in a bright green crystallized exfoliating rub. If she chased after Nana, she'd just fall flat on her face on the polished granite tile.

Not that it could hurt more than Nana's rejection.

"There's nothing to talk about. You didn't like the idea on Friday when I surprised you with coming out here. But now, even after meeting Bill, you still can only talk about how you think something's wrong with me. I know something's different, Lisa. Why do you think I want to enjoy life while I can? I don't need to go see Dr. Reynolds. I saw him two months ago. You're right. I'm in the early stages of Alzheimer's. I don't have much to look forward to. But I am looking forward to my wedding. And if you can't be happy for me while I try to live out the good days I still have, then, no, you're not welcome. I'm sorry, Lisa Marie, but that's the way it is."

Nana turned around and padded out of the Grand Florence Spa, a little unsteady. Lisa would normally blame the disposable flip-flops and their ill-fit, but she saw Nana's shoulders shake as she neared the door, and she knew her grandmother was trying to hold back her tears.

Lisa struggled to hold back her own.

When one slipped out, Lisa didn't care.

"She'll still want you there," the nail technician said quietly over the sounds of the bubbling water and massaging chair.

"I don't think so. I think this is one memory Alzheimer's will never take away from her."

Lisa knew that the day she made her Nana cry was one she'd never forget, either.

And she cursed her inability to have just kept her mouth shut and gone with the flow like Ryan told her to do. For a teacher, Lisa realized, she certainly had a hard time learning lessons.

After the lonely pedicure session ended, Lisa walked around the sprawling campus of the Renaissance Grand. She strolled through the casino, filled with bright lights and bells, as people of all ages and backgrounds staked out their favorite games, pulled levers, and watched dice tumble and waited on a flash of white, red, or black to change their fortune.

Her fortune, it seemed, had been decided. She'd been uninvited from Nana's wedding, and she'd never felt so low in her life. Not even all the times waiting at the window for a mother who never showed added up to the heartbreak she felt right now.

She'd let Nana down.

They used to be two-against-the-world. And now Nana had someone else in her life to laugh with, confide in, and live life with.

Lisa meandered to the main hallway of shops and sat heavily on a velvet-covered bench across from the boutique where Ryan had taken her on her first night in the hotel.

Slumping over, she placed her head in her hands and struggled against the bitter truth. She couldn't let go of the relationship she and Nana had always had. And in trying to keep her close, Lisa had pushed her away.

What if she'd pushed her away forever?

What if Nana stayed here in Las Vegas, leading her new life, and never came home to Port Provident again?

What if Nana never let Lisa back in her life again?

What if her Alzheimer's took a dramatic turn and Nana never even had the chance to allow Lisa back into her life?

Because, Lisa realized, the facts were simple. Nana already had a diagnosis of Alzheimer's. One she'd been hiding, apparently for months. With Alzheimer's, Lisa knew the outcome of the game before it had even been played.

She would lose Nana.

She would lose the support she'd had her whole life. She'd lose the one person who knew all her memories—her first steps, her first words, her first day of school.

The tears began to flow from the corners of Lisa's eyes and down her cheeks before she even realized they'd slipped out. Thoughts of her life with Nana, the good times, the bad times, and everything in between, continued to come, gaining speed like a race car on a track. Lisa couldn't keep up with all the memories, and she couldn't keep up with all the tears.

As the sobs choked her throat, Lisa felt thankful that her head was buried in her hands and covered by her hair. At least no one could see her.

Not that she cared. They were all relaxing on their Spring Break vacations. She was losing everything that had ever mattered to her.

She'd pushed Ryan away last night after getting caught in the limo last night.

She'd pushed Nana away, by focusing on what she wanted. She'd treated Nana, her greatest teacher in life, like nothing more than a student who needed to be told what to do.

She'd told Ryan she needed to know if she could trust him.

But now, Lisa couldn't even be trusted by the person who counted on her most.

A light hand laid on Lisa's right shoulder.

"*Cara Mia*, are you all right?"

Lisa lifted her head and wiped her eyes. Mariela, the manager of the boutique, sat on the tufted bench next to her.

"No. I'm not. I think I've lost everything." The words squeezed painfully through Lisa's choked throat, rasping as they clawed their way out.

Mariela patted Lisa's shoulder gently. "I've seen it before. You aren't the only one, *Cara Mia*."

Lisa shook her head. "You don't understand. It's not money. I haven't lost a dime of my money. I've lost my Nana."

"Come with me." Mariela put her hand under Lisa's elbow and helped her to her feet. "Let's get you out of this busy area. You can come with me to the boutique, get yourself back together in private, and we'll get someone to help with your Nana."

Lisa shuffled across the wide hallway, leaning heavily on Mariela's steadying arm. "I don't think anyone can help."

They walked through the door of the boutique, and quiet enveloped Lisa—such a contrast from the frantic to-and-fro and babble of voices in the hallway.

"There's a chair by the dressing room if you need it, or just feel free to walk around and browse. Whatever makes you the most comfortable, Lisa. I will make some calls." The gentle Italian lilt that touched Mariela's words calmed Lisa a little more. Her voice sounded soothing.

"I...I think I'll just walk around." Maybe doing something mindless like looking at dresses on the racks would take her mind off the soul-crushing feeling that continued to bore into her heart like a drill bit.

Lisa weaved her way through the racks, generally oblivious of the finery hanging on them. The whirl of thoughts wouldn't allow her to focus on anything for long.

Finally, in the back corner of the store, she looked up. A beautiful ivory wedding dress with an embroidered lace bodice and an A-line satin skirt hung in a place of honor. Lisa fingered the dress delicately, holding it out slightly so she could see it better. She twisted it slightly on the hanger so she could look at the detail on the back. A line of satin ribbon crisscrossed down the center, laced like a corset.

Her breath caught in her throat. The dress reminded her of a princess in a fairytale.

Then a sob caught in her throat as she remembered that today was Nana's wedding day—and she would not be there.

"You'd look beautiful in that, you know."

Lisa jumped at the sound of Ryan's voice.

"You scared me. What are you doing here?"

Ryan gave a hint of a smile. "Mariela called me. She said she saw you crying out in the main hallway. She was worried about you. What's wrong?"

"It's Nana. I've lost her."

"What do you mean, 'lost her'?" Ryan reached out and placed his hand around Lisa's forearm.

"We were getting a pedicure this morning and I decided to tell her how I felt. I was running out of time. She got up and left." Lisa felt her throat begin to clog with tears and memories. "And she told me not to come to the wedding."

The thick bile of regret choked her and Lisa struggled momentarily to get a breath.

"Where is she now?" Ryan's words sounded as rough as sandpaper.

Lisa could barely summon a whisper. "I don't know."

"We'll find her, Lisa."

At the sound of his declaration, Lisa felt a small ray of sunshine in the gray clouds that had chased her this morning. She'd prided herself for so long on her street-smarts: weathering the abandonment of her mother, surviving New York, building a new career for herself as a teacher. But the panic she'd felt this morning revealed all those accomplishments for what they truly were: a master class, the performance of her life.

Literally and figuratively. Her life had been a big performance and her lines had been lies she'd told herself for years to make up for the fact that she didn't trust anyone except Nana.

And now Nana had cut herself off from Lisa.

Thinking about it again, admitting the frailty of her own situation, stung like a blade skimming lightning-quick across the surface of her skin. It stung. And it bled.

And she knew it would bleed for a long time to come.

Ryan put his arm around her shoulders and squeezed. The solid, toned muscle of his bicep pressed against the crest of her shoulder blades and his forearm braced the curve of her joint and he touched the edge of her collarbone with his fingers.

No tourniquet had stopped the loss of heart's blood any more efficiently than the bracing touch of Ryan McBride.

"Ryan?" Before they left in search of Nana, Lisa urgently needed to make her peace with the other piece of the puzzle that had been troubling her.

"Yes?" He looked down but kept his arm cemented firmly around her shoulder.

"I'm sorry." She wasn't brave enough to speak it loudly, but she hoped he could sense her sincerity.

She turned her head at an upward angle and tried to search the expression on his face. All she could see was the same even, polished look he'd kept on his face both times she'd seen him in the main room at the tournament.

His game face.

She needed to make him understand this wasn't a game any longer to her. She wanted to play for keeps.

"For pushing you away last night. I've been nothing but hot and cold to you. And yet you still came when Mariela called."

"I told you, Lisa. I want you to trust me."

She could have said she didn't have any other choice. But that wouldn't have done justice to how she felt when she'd heard the sound of his voice just now, when she knew he'd come, when she knew if he was with her, everything would be all right.

"I do."

He led her out of the boutique with a quick wave to Mariela as they passed. "Save those words for later, my dear. I promise you're going to need them."

RYAN COULDN'T PINPOINT what exactly prompted him to say that to Lisa, but he couldn't dwell on it for too long. The first order of business was to get up to the honeymoon suite, find Nana, and get this misunderstanding sorted out between her and Lisa.

Seeing Lisa there in front of that wedding dress, locked on it with the full concentration of her being, made him wish the wedding occurring today would be theirs.

He'd read Lisa the moment he'd met her. She was running scared. Fear chased her like an opponent in a marathon. It dogged her every step. He'd been trained to scrutinize his opponents, to analyze their movements, and to study physical cues. As an actress, Lisa played the role of loving granddaughter and enthusiastic teacher well. But when she let her guard down—which he'd gotten her to do in the private moments they'd spent together—she stepped out of character.

Ryan had seen her for who she was—someone who loved fiercely, dreamed grandly, and fought hard to do what she perceived to be the right thing.

And he loved that fighting, dreaming streak. All of it.

Even the fact that she held herself back, but yet kissed with passion, then stepped back to analyze—or over-analyze, more accurately—the situation fascinated him. In a city full of flash and faux, it proved to him that Lisa was a real person who contemplated the consequences of her actions. She wasn't willing to risk it all on a roll of the dice.

Could he convince her to risk her heart—before it was all too late?

"I bet she's back in her suite, Lisa. You don't need to be so nervous." Ryan watched Lisa chew the tip of her fingernail into oblivion as they rode up the elevator to the suite.

She shook her head. "You didn't see her. I've never seen her that agitated."

"I've never seen you this agitated."

The doors opened and Lisa's body language replied wordlessly as she walked through the double doors. Although her hands still fidgeted, now her head bowed and her shoulders rounded forward, aging her by at least ten additional years.

In his mind's eye, Ryan saw the sassy, confident Lisa of just two days ago, strutting across the honeymoon suite in black lace and marabou feathers like she had all of Las Vegas in her hand.

That had been the walk of an accomplished actress, playing a role. In front of him now was a broken woman, a real woman, mourning what she saw as lost forever.

Both of them tore at his heart as he remembered the true Lisa—the passionate and compassionate woman who kissed like a firework and protected those she loved like a guard dog.

Lisa swiped the key card in the lock of the door and pressed down on the handle, swinging the polished wooden door open slowly and fearfully.

Once they were out of the entry, Ryan pushed gently around her right side. He could be Lisa's voice and take that burden away from her.

"Gina Mae? Are you here? It's Ryan."

His voice echoed off the marble and glass of the suite. Only silence answered back.

Lisa didn't say anything, just headed toward the bedroom, opening every door in her path and giving a cursory look inside.

"Ryan, she's not here."

Ryan's own adrenaline pulsed a little more quickly. He'd been certain Gina Mae would be back in her suite getting ready for this evening's ceremony and awaiting an olive branch from her granddaughter. But instead of Gina Mae, they were greeted only by silence.

"Ok. Let me call Pops. If she's not here, she's with him."

Ryan pulled his cell phone out of his pocket and dialed Pops. When his grandfather answered, he cut straight to the chase.

"Hey, Pops. Is Gina Mae with you?"

"No, I just woke up from a nap." The older man punctuated his sentence with a shallow yawn. "Isn't she with Lisa at the spa?"

"No." He didn't want his grandfather to worry, but he couldn't sugarcoat what was going on. "They had an argument and Gina Mae left. Lisa and I are in the suite now. She's not here."

Lisa stood at the expanse of glass at the back of the room, looking out. Her shoulders began to tremble and Ryan knew she'd begun to cry.

"Pops, just stay put and don't worry. I'll call the hotel staff. I'll take care of it. They'll find her."

"You'll call me as soon as you hear, right, Ryan?" Worry had overtaken the sleepiness in Pops' voice.

He could reassure Pops, he could reassure Lisa. He hoped he could reassure himself. "Of course, Pops. You know I will."

Ryan disconnected the call and started to dial the concierge desk like he had the other night. He hesitated, wanting to wrap Lisa in his arms first and dry her tears.

But her tears would stop for good when she knew where Nana was, and the sooner he made the call, the faster that could happen.

As soon as the attendant at the desk answered, Ryan cut off her formal answering speech. "Winter, it's Ryan McBride. I need your help again, this time to look for Gina Mae Fleming, my grandfather's fiancée. She's gone missing. Can you talk to security?"

"Certainly, Mr. McBride. Give me ten minutes and I'll call you back."

"Thanks, Winter. I appreciate it."

Ryan put the phone back in his pocket. He started to reach for Lisa, then hesitated. "They're going to find her, Lisa. Remember what I told you last time? There are a thousand eyes in this hotel. Security knows everything. No one just disappears in a Las Vegas casino."

The glassy topaz sparkle had fled from her eyes, chased away by the dull gray haze of worry. He'd lost himself in her eyes before. Now Lisa was the one who was lost. And so was Gina Mae.

Ryan knew he had to do everything in his power to rescue the older woman.

The two most important people in his life—Pops and Lisa—were counting on him.

"Ryan, what if she doesn't come back?" Lisa's shoulders shook briefly with the stifled hiccup that signaled a lingering desire to cry.

"Lisa, why wouldn't she come back? People have disagreements. They get angry. Then they work it out. Gina Mae does not seem like the kind to hold a grudge. Especially not against you."

Lisa continued to stare straight ahead, focusing her emotion on the to-and-fro so many floors below where they stood.

"Because she has Alzheimer's. I've seen stories on the news about Alzheimer's patients who get lost and can't get home. They put things like Amber Alerts out for them." Her voice wavered slightly as she talked about the idea of a warning being issued across cell phone texts, TV alerts, and highway signs.

Ryan tried to will his phone to ring with an update, but it stayed silent.

"You don't know that for sure. You won't know until you get her into a doctor. She's probably just out buying a new pair of shoes or earrings for tonight. You know, something borrowed, something blue...and all that."

Lisa turned around to face him. Fresh tear tracks snaked down her cheeks, bordered by the thinnest thread of mascara on the edges. "No, she told me this morning as she was walking away. She went to Dr. Reynolds herself months ago and kept it from me. That's why she wants to marry Bill. She wants to be happy and enjoy herself while she still can."

Ryan touched the pad of his thumb to one of Lisa's trails of tears, wiping them gently away. He wished he could wipe away her sorrow and fear as easily.

She leaned forward, falling into his chest, and he collected her in his arms, cradling her as gently as a kitten. He pulled her tight with one arm and stroked her hair rhythmically with the other, providing her a safe place to sob as her fears pushed to the surface and refused to be contained.

"We're going to find her, Lisa."

Her tears soaked circles in the front of his shirt. "We have to, Ryan. It's all my fault. It's all my fault."

"Let's go downstairs. I know the chief of security. We'll talk to him directly. We'll find her, Lisa. Whatever it takes."

Ryan felt his heart crack with each haltingly choked sob that came from Lisa.

And that's when he knew his whole world had changed.

He didn't want to marry Lisa, like he'd half-joked yesterday, because it would make their grandparents happy and would solve some problems. He didn't want a marriage of convenience just to check some boxes.

He realized he wanted a marriage of inconvenience.

Because he'd fallen in love with Lisa Fleming when he'd least expected to. And that was seriously inconvenient for a man who'd just quit his job and didn't know where he was heading with his life.

All he knew was he loved this honey-eyed woman who completely loved her Nana and her students and her belief in happily ever after.

He wanted her to love him too. She deserved her own happily ever after, and he was going to make it happen.

Neither of them grew up with a traditional family. But they had the chance to come together and create their own, with Nana and Pops too. Ryan knew whatever his next steps were, he needed to use his time and energy to make a difference.

And right now, he needed to be that difference for Lisa. He needed to be her rock. And he needed to make sure that he left no stone unturned to find Nana.

Lisa pulled back and wiped her eyes with her fingers, wiping mascara toward the side of her face. She looked like a raccoon.

But as long as she was his raccoon, Ryan didn't care.

"What are you smiling at?" Lisa sniffled as she tried to get the words out.

Ryan hesitated slightly, not knowing if this was the right time to say what was on his mind. He'd made a living taking calculated risks. And saying the right thing to Lisa right now was probably the highest-stakes event he'd ever been in.

Lisa deserved the best he could give right now, though, and that was honesty. So he decided to reply simply.

"You."

"Me?" Her shoulders squared slightly.

"You're just beautiful, that's all." He decided to deny Lisa the opportunity to protest. They had work to do. "Let's go downstairs and find Nana."

THE ELEVATOR WAS NOT descending to the lobby fast enough.

The doors were not opening fast enough.

The path down the large hallway was not clear enough.

The butterflies in her stomach were not flying away enough.

Lisa could not keep the nervous energy from shaking every fiber of her being. Her hands felt as though she'd had a cappuccino with a double shot of espresso, followed by a mochaccino chaser. Her heart raced like one belonging to a sprinter at the finish line. Her thoughts flitted around, as mixed and jumbled as a toddler's toy box.

"Ryan, I've got some information for you." An imposingly tall man in a midnight black suit waved them over as soon as they came near the concierge desk.

"Have you spotted her, McGivern?"

"Well, yes and no. Come over here to the security desk and I'll show you some of our CCTV footage."

"Lisa, this is Blake McGivern, the Renaissance's head of security." Ryan held Lisa's hand and gently directed her toward a desk near the back of the expansive lobby. As they stopped at the desk, Ryan gestured back toward Lisa with his free hand. "This is Lisa Fleming, Mrs. Fleming's granddaughter."

"Miss Fleming, we're doing everything we can to locate your grandmother. Can you tell me if the woman in this footage is her?"

Lisa leaned in toward the small TV and tried to decipher the figures on the black and white image. "That one, back there by the lounge chair on the right. That's her."

At least she thought it was. The image was small and a little grainy, and she couldn't say with one hundred percent certainty.

She knew only two things for certain right now. One, she had to find Nana—and quickly—before her heart burst from nervous adrenaline overload. And two, she didn't know how she could ever repay Ryan for his cool, yet compassionate, handling of the situation.

He'd taken control, made phone calls, directed her movements. When they found Nana, it would be largely due to Ryan's quick thinking, seemingly endless contacts and resources, and unflappable presence under pressure.

As he spoke in deliberate undertones with McGivern, Lisa forced her mind to slow enough to think about the situation from a different angle. Not the Nana angle. The Ryan angle.

In so many ways, Ryan McBride was Lisa's polar opposite. She was a drama nerd, driven by emotions and grand gestures, and a sense of scene and moment.

Ryan was deeply analytical, kept his emotions in check, and never made a move without considering the consequences.

And while her first priority was finding Nana, as Lisa watched Ryan take control of the situation with a practiced authority, she wondered what her life would be like if she lost Ryan's presence in her life too.

"Lisa? Did you hear me?" Ryan tapped her on the shoulder to get her attention.

"No, I'm sorry. My mind is wandering."

Ryan let his hand linger on her shoulder. The simple gesture gave her some grounding, some strength.

"I know. It's ok. If that woman you identified by the pool is Nana, they also have footage of her leaving the hotel."

Fear closed her throat with the breath-robbing choke of a roundhouse kick to the throat.

"Oh, dear God, please, no." The short, ineloquent prayer escaped Lisa's lips with the last bit of air she had left. Tears brimmed along the edge of her eyelids. "She doesn't know her way around Las Vegas. Where would she go? How will we find her, Ryan?"

"We've already called the police, Miss Fleming." The Renaissance Grand's head of security nodded at the officer behind the desk. "And I'm alerting the security teams at the other hotels in our immediate area. We will find her."

"He means it, Lisa. They'll find her." Ryan placed a hand on each shoulder and squared up her posture. He looked her straight in the eye.

A parade of worst-case scenarios started a relentless march through her mind. A dreamer's imagination could be a wonderful tool, or the script for an outlandish made-for-TV-style movie, full of twists and turns and fictional implausibilities that seemed real.

"Ryan, they have to."

"They will. Do you want to go back to your room and wait?"

Lisa locked her gaze straight on him. She needed him like a life preserver in a cold, battering ocean. She couldn't process all the emotions in her veins and all the thoughts that continued to whirl.

"No. Please don't leave me by myself. I just keep thinking of all these things that could happen to Nana, alone on the streets of a strange city."

"Okay. Come with me. I need to drop by the Shamrocks for Students tournament and tell NCN that I need to reschedule my interview."

Ryan's voice sounded calm and gentle. The syllables reassured Lisa. Ryan knew so many people all over this town. Lisa knew he'd use every contact he had, every string he could pull to make sure Nana returned safely.

Lisa knew she just needed to trust him.

Except for Nana, Lisa had trusted lots of people in her life, and they'd always let her down. A playboy bachelor gambler in the middle of Las Vegas didn't seem like someone to break that streak, even though she had to admit, Ryan was not the stereotype.

Still, trust didn't always come easy to Lisa, and she knew it. But Nana was alone on the streets of Las Vegas. Lisa didn't have any choice. She had to put all the faith and trust she had in Ryan's hands.

Lisa had to bet it all on Ryan.

They wound around the hotel and through the casino area before coming to an area roped off near the main auditorium where the Shamrocks for Students tournament was being held. Posters of schoolchildren lined the walls in the immediate area, larger-than-life-sized black and white images of kids working with technology, studying, and finding the spark ignited by learning. Each photograph was accented with details that had been shaded in primary colors. The pop of color drew in the eyes and Lisa found herself studying each child's face closely.

It was a welcome respite from the worry about Nana that had gnawed at the corners of her mind since she first woke up this morning and decided to use their trip to the spa to cover contentious territory.

She knew then that she'd have kicked herself for not talking to Nana about calling off the wedding.

She just didn't know how much harder she'd kick herself for the consequences of that conversation.

"This won't take long, I promise. Then we'll go check back in at the security desk and see what they've found out, and make our plan from there."

Every security team in this part of Las Vegas had been alerted to look for Nana, as had the police department.

"I know. I don't know the city or the hotels around here. There's not much I can do right now."

"It's going to be okay, Lisa." He gave her hand a light squeeze. The significance of the gentle touch felt heavy—they were in this together, a team.

Holding Ryan's hand served as a tangible reminder that she wasn't alone.

Even if she felt completely alone without Nana.

Ryan spoke quickly with an NCN producer. "All right, I'll see you back in a few hours. Thanks for understanding."

"Everything settled?" Lisa hadn't been able to keep her wandering mind focused on anything Ryan had said to the TV crew.

"They'll have to rearrange a little bit, but Tony assured me he could do it. They want an interview with me, so they may not like my terms, but they'll agree to them because it gets them ten exclusive minutes with the guy who walked away from the table. I'm the hottest story in their beat right now."

"*Mmm-hmm*." Lisa looked at a white-haired woman sitting down in front of a flamingo pink slot machine. It could have been Nana, but it wasn't.

"The hottest story in *my* beat right now, though, is finding Nana." Ryan stopped in the middle of the room. "Look at me."

Flashing lights blinked and digital music snippets played all around them. He placed one hand under Lisa's chin and turned her head slightly.

Lisa forced the fog from her mind and pulled the muscles in her eyelids up.

"I told them I had a family crisis to take care of."

"A family crisis?" Lisa pushed the words out on a shaky breath. Why had he described it that way to the TV crew?

Ryan nodded and held her hand tightly. She could feel herself trying to pull his strength through where their palms touched, so she could use it as her own.

"A family crisis. Today is the day our grandparents are getting married. We're going to find Gina Mae and she's going to marry Pops and achieve her goal of having the best life she can in the time she has left to enjoy it. And you and I are going to enjoy life right alongside them. We are all in this together, Lisa."

Lisa's throat tightened like the grip of a Venus flytrap on an unsuspecting insect. She swallowed hard, trying to open up the passage so she could breathe.

The only words strong enough to battle through to the surface were those of her deepest fear.

"What happens when she fades away and no longer knows who I am, Ryan?"

"The heart never forgets, Lisa." The blue of his eyes was as open as the sea where it meets the sky to form the horizon. She looked closely and saw the edge of forever in them. "And when the mind does, I'll be there with you."

Ryan leaned over and touched his lips to hers, a gentle kiss that punctuated his statement with a language her heart would understand long after her own mind had forgotten most of what had happened today. Lisa allowed herself to fold into Ryan to pull even more of his strength to her, to give her the support she so desperately needed. As she did, she felt the weight that had dragged behind her since childhood fall away.

Ryan met her wordless invitation, deepening the kiss, and as Lisa opened her mouth slightly, she felt a gentle river of emotion push through her veins and open her heart as well.

She'd spent far too long being lonely. But her heart told her that if she'd just believe in Ryan, she wouldn't be alone, no matter what lay ahead.

"She's been found." Blake McGivern waved Ryan down as soon as he and Lisa stepped into the lobby.

Lisa felt relief wash over her like the downpour of the waterfall at the back of the Renaissance Grand's resort-style pool.

Only two things mattered to Lisa right now...that Nana was safe, and that she would be happy.

"Oh, thank you, God. And thank you, Mr. McGivern." Lisa's prayers had been answered. And she had Ryan's quick thinking and connections to thank for the early intervention that brought Nana back quickly and without incident.

"Where was she, Blake?" Ryan cupped a hand around Lisa's shoulder, a side hug full of happy emotions.

"Next door at the Palazzo. She'd gone to the spa over there to finish her pedicure."

Of course, she had. Because while Lisa had held misgivings about the wedding, there had never been any doubt in Nana's mind that she would marry Bill today. Nana had always been one for quiet determination. Once she set herself on a path, nothing caused her to waver.

Once it had become clear that Lisa's father's medical issues would prevent him from being an engaged parent, and once it had become clear that Lisa's mother wasn't coming back, Nana had never wavered. She stepped in and acted in the role of father, mother, and great-grandmother. Unconditional love and a backbone of steel. Nana had always possessed both in bushels.

Lisa knew she needed to repay her grandmother with nothing less than the same.

"Let's go get her, Ryan. We have a wedding to prepare for."

McGivern listened to something coming through his clear earpiece. "No need. The Palazzo security staff is escorting her back here. She should be back shortly."

"Thanks again, man." Ryan reached his hand out toward McGivern and shook the security officer's hand heartily. "I appreciate it. Lisa, do you want to go back to the suite and wait for her, and I'll call Pops?"

She shook her head, nervous energy fueling her movements. "No. I'm going to wait right here. I have something to say to her, and I don't want to wait."

"Ok, well, let's go over to the couches by the door, then."

Ryan led Lisa over to a grouping of red leather couches just off to the left of the main entrance area. Lisa tapped her left foot in a random pattern, ticking off the seconds.

Ryan rested a hand lightly on her knee. The arch of his palm curved over her kneecap and Lisa couldn't help but notice how it seemed to fit perfectly.

Finally, after a few minutes, the oversized sliding glass doors opened and a black-uniformed man guided Nana inside and turned toward the security desk.

"Nana!"

Lisa leaped up and covered the distance between them in mere seconds. She gathered Nana in her arms as though she were a child's prized teddy bear and squeezed. She never wanted to let go.

Tears began to trickle over the paper-thin skin of Nana's cheeks.

"Don't cry, Nana. This is all my fault."

"I shouldn't have gotten so angry, sweetheart."

Lisa jumped in before Nana could speak any further. This was her apology and she wanted to fully own it. The responsibility fell squarely on her shoulders.

"It's okay, Nana. I was wrong and I'm sorry. I felt like what I was doing was right. I promise I've only tried to do what I felt was right for you. But I need to trust you and respect your decisions. And I respect why you want to marry Bill. I was scared, and I felt you weren't thinking through your decision.

I was scared that I was going to lose you—both mentally and physically, too, if you stayed out here."

Nana gave a powerful sniff to stop the parade of saltwater droplets. "Then I raised you right. I raised a girl who loves mightily and cares enough to do what she feels is right, even when it's tough."

Lisa didn't quite know what to say. Nana's approval felt better than any critic's review or any red carpet she could walk or any gold statue for which she could give an acceptance speech.

"I wish I'd told you about all this weeks ago so we could have worked this out before things ever came to this. I accept your apology, Lisa Marie. Will you accept mine?"

She buried her head in Nana's shoulder and tightened the bear hug. "Always, Nana. I love you."

"I love you too, Lisa Marie. Now, can I ask you something one more time?"

"Sure." Lisa pulled back and looked at Nana, wondering just what she was getting at.

"I asked you the other day and you didn't answer. You said you were going to get me a dementia test. Now that we know that test is out of the way, I still need a maid of honor. Will you stand up with me when I marry Bill?"

Lisa couldn't keep the tears from welling up. She nodded her assent, momentarily unable to speak. "Of course, Nana. There's nothing I'd like more."

After they'd gotten everything sorted out with the security team, Lisa and Nana left Ryan and went to the Renaissance Grand's wedding chapel, where the wedding ceremony would take place later this evening.

Nana gave one last signature on the checklist she'd been handed by the hotel's wedding coordinator, confirming all the details. She handed it back to the coordinator with a smile.

"I think everything's settled. Except for one thing." Nana looked at Lisa with a sideways glance.

Lisa couldn't think of any more burdens that needed to be lifted. "What?"

"Well, you and Ryan, of course."

Nana laid her words out with a matter-of-fact finality, forcing Lisa to realize she wasn't sweet-talking her way out of answering.

Except that she didn't know what the answer was.

In fact, she wasn't one-hundred-percent sure even what the question was.

"What about me and Ryan, Nana?" Lisa held her breath slightly while waiting for Nana's clarification.

"Don't act like you don't know what I'm talking about, Lisa Marie."

Lisa shook her head at the admonishment. "But I really don't know what you're talking about, Nana."

"I've seen you through a few relationships. Some good. Some bad. And then there was that two-faced jerk you were engaged to for a while. But I've never seen you let your guard down so quickly with someone."

"Well, you know what they say, Nana. What happens in Vegas..."

"They say it stays in Vegas. So, are you going to go back to Port Provident and let Ryan stay in Vegas?" Nana sat on the front pew in the chapel.

"Well, I can't stay here. I've got a few more days of Spring Break, but that's it until summer. I have a teaching contract. I can't just quit and never go back."

"What strings does Ryan have tying him down? He quit his job. Why don't you ask him to come with you?"

"You want me to ask him to leave the lights of Las Vegas for Port Provident? I just can't see anyone trading all this for humidity and seagull poop on your car."

Besides, she needed Ryan close to Nana and Bill. Lisa needed to know someone was there to take care of them since she would be hundreds of miles away.

She wouldn't be able to sleep at night if Ryan wasn't in the same place as Nana and Pops.

Of course, she'd be doing plenty of tossing and turning thinking about this Spring Break to remember—and the man she'd never forget, the one who had taught her to be more spontaneous, to trust in her instincts, and to not be afraid to take a gamble on life every now and then.

"You never know until you ask, Lisa Marie. Remember where you got with not asking me about my plans with Bill and your suspicions about how my brain was—or wasn't—working."

Lisa frowned at the recent, biting memory. That shoe fit. And it was way too tight.

"But what would I say, Nana? Hey, I've known you for less than a week...wanna run off with me to the paradise of Port Provident, Texas?"

"That doesn't sound appealing at all." Nana tsk-tsked with her tone of voice.

"Exactly. It sounds crazy. Which is what it is."

Nana reached up and took Lisa's hand in her own, the swirls of her fingertips softened and worn down by more than nine decades of living. It felt like the touch of a velvet teddy bear, holding on tightly to a dream.

"No. What's crazy is not listening to your heart and watching someone walk out of your life, possibly forever. You don't have to deal with World War II, but this is one lesson you need to make sure you learn from me."

Lisa paused, conflicted by Nana's words. "But Nana, I still don't understand something. If you hadn't gone your separate ways back then, you wouldn't have me. Bill wouldn't have Ryan. If you erase the mistakes of your past, then you erase me."

Nana's fingers squeezed the edges of Lisa's palm tightly. "That's when it all comes down to faith. Knowing that God works out our lives the way they're supposed to. But that doesn't mean we abdicate responsibility for making thoughtful decisions, or just throw our lives to the wind like a boomerang and hope it comes back to us."

Something about Nana's words slowed the whirling thoughts in Lisa's mind. She'd been guilty of not always making the most thoughtful decisions.

"But what should I do, Nana?"

She remembered being a child, sitting at the window at the front of her house, waiting on her mother to come home, and asking Nana the same question. *What should I do?*

Lisa didn't want to waste her life waiting and wishing and hoping. She'd done that as a child because that was the only course of action she knew to take. This time, she knew better.

Nana patted Lisa on the hand, always a steady presence in her life.

"Follow your heart."

Chapter Eight

RYAN HEADED BACK TOWARD the NCN TV set at the Shamrocks for Students tournament.

Before Mariela had summoned him to Lisa's side, he'd had the chance to spend the morning talking to the head of the Cutting Edge Students charity, the recipients of the funds raised through the tournament. Their mission was to raise money to support new and innovative ideas in education around the country.

Ryan thought back to the conversation he'd had this morning.

"A lot of times districts have ideas to improve access to certain types of education, or to bring a completely new program to kids, but they don't have the funding to sustain it," Jim Palmer, the charity's president, told Ryan. "That's where we come in. We raise funds to support these programs and the districts and teachers who are thinking out of the box. Then we give it to them as grant money. Big tournaments like the Shamrocks for Students event are our bread and butter, but not everything we do is as much of a splash as this. Little things, day in and day out across the country add up to make a difference too."

They'd gone over a list of things that the Cutting Edge Students Foundation had done and their plans for the year ahead. Thinking about the conversation he'd had with Jim started Ryan's mind racing again. Jim had clearly laid out the dots that needed to be connected to accomplish their goals.

What Ryan had appreciated the most about their conversation was the enthusiasm Jim had for the students he served. It had reminded Ryan of how animated Lisa had been the other night in their booth in the piano bar.

She'd shared all about her students and the passion she'd found for teaching once she'd left her dreams of stage and spotlight behind. Lisa's sincere joy in that whole evening forced him to see her from a totally different perspective.

And as this wedding weekend had continued to bring them together, that perspective had grown sharper and sharper. He had more questions than answers right now about where he was going and what he wanted out of his life, but he knew he didn't want to lose Lisa's place in it.

Of all the risks he'd taken over the years, losing Lisa wasn't one he was willing to take.

And he wasn't content to just be her step-whatever-relative when their grandparents married.

It wasn't good enough.

But how could he convince her that the only jackpot he wanted to win was her heart?

"Ryan!" Tony Collins, the lead producer for NCN's coverage of the Shamrocks for Students tournament, waved in his direction, breaking the Lisa-induced fog which had completely surrounded his thoughts on the walk over here.

He'd been on complete auto-pilot through the halls of the Renaissance Grand.

Love would do that to you, he guessed.

Love.

He'd begun to realize it when he was teasing Lisa yesterday as they were getting out of the limo. It had come on quickly, but strangely, it didn't even cause him the slightest hesitation to reinforce that in his mind—and in his heart.

He just didn't know what to do about it. He knew Lisa appreciated his help earlier today, and even seemed to enjoy the time they'd spent together—when she'd finally let her guard down. But he'd be fooling himself if he thought she'd come to the same conclusions he had.

"You ready, Lucky Charm?" Emma Brown swiveled in her chair to face him.

"I told you, Emma. The name's just Ryan. Ryan McBride. The poker player is retired. And the name is retiring with him."

"Aww, that's no fun." She pushed her lower lip into a slight pout. "I guess I'll just have to play along."

He wouldn't miss this kind of nonsense, of every woman in Las Vegas trying to flirt with him. "I guess you will, Emma."

The pout faded and she rolled her eyes slightly at Ryan. Too bad for Emma and her years of trying to come on to him—but the only eyes he had time for now, sparkled like warm honey. Lisa had never tried to come on to him. Even when she'd found out that he'd won some tournaments and had a bank account to go along with that, she'd never treated him differently.

Emma adjusted her cotton candy pink leather skirt and fluffed her blonde hair, arranging the front corkscrew curls just so, placing them over each shoulder with a practiced hand.

"Tony, let me know when you're ready to start."

"In about two minutes, Em. The second-to-last round is almost over. We'll cut to you and Ryan at the break between rounds." Tony took off his headphones and looked at Ryan. "I saw you talking with Jim Palmer earlier, Ryan. What was that all about?"

"I ran into him earlier and he was telling me about some of the things the foundation is doing. This is a tournament that does a lot of good, you know. It's something I think more people need to know about."

"Want Jim to join you for part of the interview? He's supposed to be stopping by soon."

Ryan nodded. He may have dropped out of the tournament, but he could definitely still help Jim spread the word about the goals of the Cutting Edge Students Foundation and try and motivate people to get involved beyond sitting at home and watching some guys play cards on TV.

"Let's do it, Tony. See if you can get him over here. That sounds like a much better interview than me talking about myself."

Tony waggled his pointer finger. "Oh, you're not getting off that easily, McBride—see, I remembered. We've got plenty of questions for you. Our Twitter feed blew up after you announced your retirement, then when you cut your stay in the tourney short...well, you wouldn't believe it. You were trending on Twitter for hours."

"So, you're saying I'm trendy?" Ryan sat down in the seat next to Emma. A staffer adjusted microphones nearby and another came by and brushed powder on his forehead. A small army clustered around Emma and made sure she was camera-ready as well.

"I'm saying you're something else, man. I don't think there have been that many poker players with that kind of effect in the last few years."

Ryan had been so consumed with Lisa and everything surrounding Pops and Gina Mae that he'd stayed largely off his phone. He hadn't seen Facebook or Twitter or his email in days. And he rarely ever pulled up a news page. He'd never been one to read the reviews, lest he find himself buying into the hype. He'd always thought of it as a competitive advantage—he'd just wanted to stay neutral and do his thing when and where it counted—at the tables.

But this week, he'd been even more cut off than ever. The only opinions he'd cared about belonged to Pops, as Ryan tried to get to know Gina Mae so he could do right by the man who'd raised him.

And then there'd been Lisa.

There just wasn't much room for nameless, faceless people providing their opinions on a computer in one-hundred-forty characters or less.

Tony waved Jim over, said a few words to him, then directed him to the chair closest to Ryan.

"Good to see you again, Jim." Ryan put his hand out to shake Jim's hand.

"Me too. I'm looking forward to continuing our conversation and spreading the message further." The older gentleman's handshake was hearty. Ryan felt the same instant comfort and connection he had when they'd spoken earlier.

"Ok, we're coming back from commercial in forty-five seconds. Everyone ready? On my count, Emma." Tony stepped into position next to a stationary camera. Ryan nodded. Emma barely moved her head, seemingly afraid to adjust the carefully-arranged curls.

Tony's fingers counted down and gave the signal for the interview to begin.

Three.

Two.

One.

Ryan had no idea what was coming in Emma's interview, but he'd get through it. Besides contributing his entry fee with no chance of earning it back, he saw this as one very tangible way he could make it up to the Foundation for retiring thirty-six hours earlier than planned.

He needed to finish his run in Vegas on good terms, then move on to the next chapter.

Whatever that might be.

Maybe he could talk to Jim a little more after the interview. Maybe he could catch some of that man's enthusiasm.

And maybe he could catch Lisa Fleming's heart.

Somehow, he couldn't see his future without a good dose of either—both Lisa and the chance to change someone else's luck instead of his own for a change.

NANA DIDN'T EVEN TWITCH.

Nothing about her demeanor even signaled a case of bridal nerves. No eyelid tics, no deep breaths, no tell-tale beads of perspiration. She was as calm and collected as always.

Same old unflappable Nana.

Lisa wished she could say the same about herself.

The ethereal sounds of Pachelbel's *Canon in D* began to play from the back of the intimate chapel.

Two fingers pushed on the spine at the small of Lisa's back. "That's your cue."

The wedding coordinator sent Lisa down the aisle. Lisa looked ahead but tried to keep her thoughts on her feet.

Step one-together. Step two-together. Step one-together. Step two-together.

The rhythm of the formal style of walking kept her thoughts off what was waiting for her at the end of the aisle.

Ryan McBride.

Lisa's gaze lifted, and she intended to look only at the spot to which she was walking. But Ryan caught her eye like a magnet pulling toward true north. Her gaze was locked. All she could do now was hope her staring wasn't too obvious. And that she didn't trip over her own feet.

Ryan's hair had been neatly smoothed back, as usual, and the shine of the overhead lights made it look as though he'd styled it with a little bit of gel. He had dressed formally, as befit the role of best man, and his tuxedo accentuated broad shoulders and a long body that just hinted at a healthy relationship with the gym, filling out and supporting the suit in a way that emphasized what Lisa could tell was an expensive fabric, made perfect through expert tailoring.

Ryan's eyes were dark, and he smiled as he noticed her gaze. White teeth that could have come straight out of a toothpaste ad stood out among the dusting of dark five o'clock shadow that covered his cheeks and chin. The longer he smiled, the more pronounced his left dimple became.

In short, Lisa decided, as she slowed her steps in advance of the altar, Ryan McBride put the sin in Sin City.

Sinfully good-looking, that is.

Ryan put his arm out, then looped it through the crook of hers.

Lisa worried that she would melt, and it wouldn't be the dramatic overhead lighting to blame.

"It's not polite to outshine the bride, you know," Ryan whispered in her ear. Lisa listened for a note of sarcasm, a short laugh. But she couldn't hear it. He sounded completely serious.

"*Sssh*." Lisa turned her head to face forward. She made herself focus on the cream-colored roses and delicate white freesia that filled the wall sconces behind the altar. Below them, on a hip-height table were groupings of navy, baby blue, and ivory candles. Their glow and the faint perfume of the flowers gave the chapel a comfortable, cherished look.

Lisa's surroundings, however, were at direct odds with the pit of her stomach. It dipped and fluttered as Ryan's arm stayed intertwined with her own as he helped her up the stairs and saw her to her assigned spot on the side of where the bride would soon be standing.

He slid his arm away, but his hand trailed over the curve of her waist. No one else would have noticed the half-second hesitation except Lisa.

But she couldn't ignore the prickle of her skin where Ryan's hand had traced, nor could she ignore the tingle that ran up and down her spine.

As the music changed and loudly announced the procession of the bride, Lisa had to make herself turn and face the aisle instead of following Ryan's footsteps back with her eyes.

Once she saw Nana, though, she couldn't think of anything other than how radiant her great-grandmother looked. Nana wore a simple, ivory suit. The candlelight ivory dupioni silk dress gathered across the waist in a criss-cross, emphasizing Nana's petite figure. Over the dress, she wore a coordinating, knee-length coat, left open to show off the dress. The collar of the coat had been embroidered with crystals and rhinestones and pearls.

In the candlelit room, it looked like a mantle of snow and ice had passed by Nana and dusted the collar of her elegant dress.

She looked every inch the radiant bride, and Lisa's heart began to glow along with the candles in the chapel and Nana's own cheeks and eyes.

Lisa had never seen Nana look happier, more proud...or younger.

And she knew, at that moment, that this was right. Nana deserved her fairytale. She deserved that and so much more. Lisa turned her head and looked at Bill. His smile was wide, with just a touch of nervousness in the lines around his eyes.

Nana deserved the world, and this man had waited almost a whole lifetime to give it to her.

"Dearly beloved..." the preacher began as Nana took her spot at the altar.

Lisa tried to focus on the preacher's words. She knew she had one more important role to play before Bill and Nana became one in the eyes of God.

Before she knew it, the moment had arrived. "Who gives this woman in marriage?"

Lisa tried to speak, but for the first time, all her years of training had failed her. She'd never missed a cue, and it had been years since she'd flubbed a line. But the seriousness of the moment fell upon her in a way that playing a role on stage had never meant to her.

She couldn't just give her Nana away. They were a team.

The frog in her throat pushed against the cartilage rings of her windpipe, making her even more aware of how conflicted and heart sore this very second in time made her.

She opened her mouth, but the words just wouldn't come.

"Her great-granddaughter and I give these two people to each other." Ryan's baritone rang true in the acoustics of the small wedding hall.

She nodded in agreement and the motion dislodged a small tear from the inner corner of Lisa's eye. She felt the warm trail down the side of the bridge of her nose.

But most of all, she felt part of something greater than herself.

She felt part of a real family, of a unit that was now more than just her and Nana against the world.

She felt love.

And when the groom finally kissed his bride, Lisa stole a look instead at the best man.

Follow her heart, Nana had said earlier. Learn from Nana's example. As Ryan again slipped his arm in the crook of Lisa's so they could follow the new Mr. and Mrs. McBride back down the aisle, Lisa couldn't help but think of a silly fantasy.

One where she followed her heart back down this very aisle, then left the chapel as another Mrs. McBride.

"THAT'S ALL YOU BROUGHT?" Ryan suspiciously eyed the bag the porter had brought up to the penthouse in the Renaissance Grand residential tower.

Lisa shrugged. "I didn't pack. Nana did. I just got handed a ticket as soon as I walked in the door from school and was told we were getting on a plane."

"Steve, you can take that to the guest room. Second door on the left down that hall." Ryan pointed to the arch at the far side of the open-floorplan living area.

The uniformed man picked up the small maroon suitcase and carried it with ease toward the room where Lisa would be staying. When he came back, Ryan pressed a few bills into his palm. "Thanks, Steve. Appreciate it."

"Certainly, Mr. McBride." Steve had been a fixture at the residential tower even longer than Ryan had. He was easy to work with and never complained.

The penthouse door shut behind Steve with a metallic click. Ryan shoved his hands in his pockets, unsure of what to say next. Neither he nor Lisa had planned on this arrangement, but of course, the newlyweds wanted to enjoy the honeymoon suite in private. Anticipating time alone with his bride, Pops had canceled his reservation and it had quickly been snatched up by an attendee of a medical industry conference that was taking over the Renaissance Grand for the upcoming week.

He didn't know why he felt nervous, like a student asking his crush to prom. The penthouse stretched for several thousand square feet. He had a spacious master suite on one side, and the guest room was all the way on the other side of his home. They wouldn't even have to cross each other's path for the rest of the night if they didn't want to.

The problem with the bravado he was trying to sell to himself was that it wasn't what he wanted.

Lisa was under his roof, and he wanted to cross paths with her. It was still early by Vegas standards, and he wanted to watch the Vegas skyline with her until the dawn peeked at the edge of the horizon. He wanted to hold her tight in the middle of the floor and sway to a jazz standard, since Pops and Gina Mae had opted for a post-ceremony dinner, instead of a reception with any kind of dancing.

He wanted whatever he could get, for as long as he could get it.

And after a few years of being one of the highest rollers in Vegas, Ryan was used to getting what he wanted.

As he watched her walk across the living room and toward the hall leading to the guest bedroom, he studied the hug of her bridesmaid's dress along her curves and the gentle sway of her hips and how her honey and flax curls hung down to the center of her back, then popped and bounced as she walked.

When she disappeared around the corner, Ryan felt a small cut from the metallic blade of fear. He'd been craving the next big thing in his life for a while now. It was why he quit the tour—to test out new waters, find a new adventure.

And now that he knew exactly what he wanted and where he wanted to go, it scared him that Lisa was going to get on a plane, head back to Texas, and that would be it. They'd see each other at Christmas with Nana and Pops, likely. But that wasn't good enough anymore. He'd realized that earlier today.

"Lisa? Do you need anything?" Ryan called around the corner. He needed to do something, to keep his mind from wandering down the path it was on.

Because girls like Lisa Fleming didn't get caught up in the Vegas myth. They didn't leave what happened in Vegas behind in Vegas. And they certainly didn't head to the legendary wedding chapel with someone they'd only known for days.

Shake out of it, McBride. You don't either. Just because you've made some changes in your life doesn't mean you've changed who you are. You don't do any of those things either.

Lisa came back to the doorway. "Actually, yes."

She looked at him with a lopsided grin paired with a sheepish shrug.

"I'd thought of changing out of this formal wear and putting on something a little more comfortable, but it seems that the hook at the top of the zipper is stuck. Do you think you could get it for me?"

He hoped hadn't lost the ability to keep his thoughts from taking up residence across his face. Because Lisa didn't need to know his mind wasn't stopping with the simple metal loop on the back of her dress.

That dress brought out the best in her.

He couldn't decide if it brought out the best—or the worst—in him.

Ryan held out his hand. He couldn't not help her. And if he indulged himself just a little bit in the process, well...

She walked over and turned her back toward him. The hook and eye came apart easily. A thread from the seam had somehow gotten wrapped around the hook. His fingers didn't move. With almost no effort, he could put the flat metal tongue of the zipper between his thumb and forefinger and tug.

That would probably be helpful, he thought to himself. Most women he knew had always said that zippers in the back were a struggle.

They'd never been a problem for him, though.

"You didn't have to..." Lisa's words trailed off as the zipper trailed down. She raised a hand and laid it on the silky fabric, trying to hold the crest of the dress up on her shoulder.

The room was silent and Ryan could hear the slight rasp of her fingertips moving across the fabric as he gently brushed her hand aside.

"Ryan, I didn't come to stay with you for this."

He adjusted his hands and guided her gently to face him. "I didn't invite you to stay for this."

Her lashes veiled her eyes. She looked up at him, but he couldn't see the irises. Couldn't get a read on what shade of honey they took on, what kind of feelings they were hiding.

A lot of women had thrown themselves at him over the years, all desperate for one night with the champion. They were all in it for the power, the prestige, the sense of high rolling.

Lisa's hesitation confirmed what Ryan already knew. She wasn't in it for any of that. In fact, her shallow breaths and the gentle cross of her arms, tucking the material up at a modest point, told him all he needed to know about Lisa.

In a city full of fake, she was real. In a city full of people who only lived once, she considered the consequences. In a city full of women he could have, she was the one he wanted.

Ryan slid his arms around Lisa's and ran five fingers down her spine and tangled the other five in her hair. He pulled her close and he lowered his head to hers.

LISA HAD LEFT HER ISLAND home and come to Las Vegas. She never expected herself to drown in the desert.

But yet, here she was, drowning in Ryan's kiss. Everything about him pulled her in. From the moment she'd locked eyes on him in the airport, she knew there was something different about him. Something edgy. Something dangerous.

She didn't know then that the true danger would be the effect of Ryan on her heart.

Because as much as she wanted to lose herself in the waves of this moment, there were other waves calling her.

The waves of Port Provident.

She had to go back.

Tomorrow. There was a plane ticket with her name on it and a classroom of students waiting for her once Spring Break was over.

This almost fairy-tale-like attraction to Ryan couldn't be denied, but then, neither could the strong pull of her real life. This wasn't going to work, and she needed to speak up before it ruined the friendship she and Ryan had built—a friendship they would both need in order to support and care for Nana and Pops in the years to come. She couldn't blow that on a few hours of indulgence that were completely incompatible with the fact that she and Ryan lived half a country apart and led very different lives.

"Ryan, I need you…" she started to say, hesitating as she pulled out of the kiss.

He jumped in at the pause. "I know."

She hadn't gotten the rest of the words out fast enough and could feel another mess brewing. This conversation could not go as badly as the pedicure chat with Nana. "Wait, let me finish."

Lisa summoned all the strength she had to take a step backward. She pulled in a deep breath, trying to clear her head as quickly as she could.

Ryan's face went dark. His jaw tightened.

"I need you here. In Las Vegas. I have a plane ticket home tomorrow. I live on the beach. You live in the desert. We're worlds apart. Realistically, I don't know how to make things work between us. I've tried to come up with some kind of plan that keeps us together, that keeps what we're coming to feel for each other alive. But I can't. I have an obligation to my kids. We have a spring play coming up at the start of April. They've worked for months on this. I can't let them down. I have to go home."

"But?"

Ryan didn't give Lisa anything to go on. She couldn't tell if he understood or if he hated her for ruining the moment and what might have been.

"But I need to know you're here. Taking care of Nana and Pops. Helping them get settled into married life together. Finding Nana the right doctors and specialists out here. She's starting a whole new life in a whole new place—but at the same time, we know what's coming. I need to know she's going to be okay and that someone is looking out for the details. You know the details. You told me so yourself. Calculating odds is taking care of the details. You're the only one who can do this for me. I trust you, Ryan."

Lisa could feel her heart slamming into her chest with each word. Never before had so much ridden on the words coming out of her mouth.

And this time, there was no role. No supporting cast. No script.

Just Lisa.

A woman who knew she loved Ryan McBride...but had to love her duty to those who counted on her more. She couldn't trade a few days with Ryan for the year with her students or the lifetime with Nana.

But would he understand? She couldn't tell.

Was this what it felt like to put everything on the table and go all-in on one hand of cards? This crazy mix of adrenaline and shortened breaths and the hope that everything would be okay?

"So you're giving up on us?"

Lisa wanted to shake her head and tell him no—if only to convince herself that somehow, somewhere, there was a chance.

But there wasn't.

At least not that she could see right now.

Nana and Pops needed someone here. Lisa couldn't be here. But Ryan could. And that's all there was to it.

"I know the ads basically say this is the place where you can forget it all. But I just can't. Too many people are depending on me."

Ryan shifted his weight from his left foot to his right, the first time he'd made any kind of motion. Too bad Lisa didn't know what that tell meant.

"And what about you? What are you depending on? You aren't on the outside looking in, you know. It's your life, Lisa."

His words hit hard. In a perfect world, she knew she'd grab Ryan's hand. They'd run down to the boutique and grab the white dress on the front rack and then they'd go straight to the closest, cheesiest wedding chapel—and spend the rest of their lives figuring out what might come next.

But even Ryan—with his years of focus on odds and outcomes—would have to admit that was more fantasy than forever.

"I'm depending on you, Ryan. Please."

Ryan walked across the room and picked up his black jacket and put it on.

"I'll take care of Nana and Pops. You know I will. There's no question about that."

Lisa thought her heart rate would slow as soon as she knew Ryan would be here for Nana. But it didn't. Adrenaline continued to prick and fizz through her veins and her fingertips; like someone had shaken a soda can then let it explode inside.

Ryan turned toward the door. Lisa's heart rate picked up even more. He couldn't be leaving. This was his house.

"But remember this, Lisa. You were wrong when you came here to stop your great-grandmother's wedding. And you're wrong now too."

Chapter Nine

"LISA, HAVE YOU HEARD a word that I've said?" Amanda Marsh looked at her co-worker with an exasperated look that she usually saved for students texting in class.

"Fine, no. I haven't." Lisa scooped up a handful of curly hair and twisted it around, securing it with several bobby pins. She leaned forward toward the makeup mirror and plucked a few curls out of the twist to fall softly around her face. "I just don't want to go."

"You're singing show tunes tonight. You can't get out of it." Amanda rifled through a drawer of stage makeup and pulled out a bright red lipstick, then handed it to Lisa.

"I could break my leg."

Amanda rolled her eyes. "That's an expression, Fleming. No one actually expects a performer to come to grievous bodily harm. It's been two months since Spring Break. You can let yourself have a little fun, you know?"

Lisa traced the lipstick around her mouth. Just the mere mention of Spring Break made her want to go into her office and shut the door. "It's not that, Amanda."

"Then what is it? You haven't been the same all semester. Tonight is supposed to be fun and supporting the STEM Academy."

"I forgot about this one—that'll teach me to not write things in my planner. It's fine. I just had plans tonight." Sure, those plans involved chocolate ice cream and a few episodes of true crime shows, but Amanda didn't need to know the details—best friend or not.

"Plans? You have ducked out of plans regularly since Spring Break. Now that the spring show is over, you can't use that as an excuse anymore." Amanda sat in the chair next to Lisa and picked up a tube of mascara. "Have you heard anything from Ryan lately? Wasn't Nana supposed to go in for some tests this week?"

Lisa slowly began to clean up the makeup she'd pulled from the drawer. "She did. She's going to call me next week with the results."

"But Ryan hasn't called?" Amanda put down the mascara and started digging through the many shades of lipstick.

"No. And why would he?" Lisa threaded a gold hoop earring through her ear.

"I don't know. Because he thinks about you as much as you think about him?"

Lisa turned and stared straight at Amanda, who had pulled her lips into the perfect pout for lipstick application. "He does not. And I don't either."

Amanda raised an eyebrow as she stared into the oversized mirror. "Didn't your Nana teach you not to lie? Speaking of poker night, you do not have a poker face, Lisa. It's a good thing you're singing tonight and not playing."

"I miss him," Lisa said simply, not knowing how her best friend would react to the declaration.

"Of course you do. I see it every day on your face." Amanda replaced the cap on the lipstick. "What did you say he said to you as he left the suite that night?"

"He'd look after Nana and Pops like I asked." She had never been so sad about someone doing exactly what she asked them to do.

Amanda pushed the chair back from the makeup table and stood up, reaching over to the switch to turn off the lights that framed the mirror. "Not that. The last part."

"I was wrong." There was no sense in embellishing or trying to provide further explanation. At this point, it was all water under the bridge. Two months had gone by. They'd barely talked—and certainly hadn't spoken of anything beyond Nana's basic care.

"You were, you know."

Lisa flipped the switch on the set of lights closest to her. "So what if I was? It doesn't change anything. I have a life here. He has a life there. Someone has to look out for Nana and Pops."

"School's almost out for the summer." Amanda's voice took on a sing-song quality that grated on Lisa's nerves.

"I'm teaching drama camp in summer school. I have medical bills to pay off from Nana's doctor appointments before she left town. I need the money."

Amanda picked up her thin black clutch handbag. "You need to call Ryan."

"Look, Amanda. I'm really glad that everything is working out so well for you and Luke. But it's just going to be like that for me. Let's just go on and go to the event. The sooner I get there, the sooner I can sing and then go home."

Amanda started to hum a tune under her breath as they walked out of the backstage area at the Port Provident High School theater. "I wanna go home with the armadillo…"

Lisa couldn't even hear the rest of the refrain. Her heart squeezed tight. She remembered that night under the stars by the pool at the Renaissance Grand. She told Ryan she wasn't his fiancée. She told him she wanted to go home. She told him she didn't want to be there.

Now, there was no place else in the world that she wanted to be than in his arms again, under the stars, like the last words between them in the penthouse had never been said.

She no longer wanted to be home with the armadillo.

She wanted to be home with Ryan. With Nana and Pops. With her family. But they all seemed to be doing fine without her in Las Vegas.

Her students still needed her, though.

And so here she would stay.

With the armadillos of Texas instead of the Lucky Charm of Las Vegas.

RYAN LIKED THE SETUP for tonight's event, a little local B&B called Provident Hill. He'd been asked to step in at the last minute for this STEM Academy fundraiser with the Cutting Edge Students charity. But Jim Palmer had come down with the flu, so Ryan hopped on a plane this morning.

It felt strange to be in Port Provident, knowing Lisa was somewhere on this island. Ryan had thrown himself into his new role as Director of Development for Cutting Edge, going around the country trying to help schools fundraise for science, math, and technology education. He loved the new job. It was creative, filled with purpose and meeting new people, and still kept him connected to the Shamrocks for Students tournament.

Now, it brought him to Lisa Fleming's backyard.

He should have called her on the drive to the airport to let her know about today's plans. But then he wouldn't have been able to stop himself from asking her to pull that little black dress with the feathers out of her closet and to be his date for the night.

And he wouldn't let himself do that. She'd made it clear that last night in Vegas where things stood. She wasn't comfortable with gambling her future on him and the lightning-quick sparks they'd found together.

He didn't like it, but as he walked alone with his thoughts around every square inch of the Renaissance Grand that night, he came to accept it. In fact, without that walk, he wouldn't have run into Jim Palmer and he wouldn't have this new direction in his life.

So, he had Lisa to thank for that. The least he could do was respect that she just didn't want any more changes in her life. She simply wanted her Nana taken care of. He admired her loyalty, even if it meant that was as far as the daydreams in his mind about what might have been could ever go.

"Thanks for coming out tonight, Ryan." A man in a sport coat put out his hand. "I'm Luke Baker, head of the new science department for the new STEM Academy. And this is Philip Bell—he is the architect on the new campus."

"It's nice to meet you both. The Foundation is looking forward to a continued partnership to make this new high school an asset to the community and the students. Have you started working on your wish list for the labs? I know that's what we're raising money here for tonight."

Luke nodded. "My list gets longer by the day. I'm a former research chemist-turned-teacher, so there are so many tools I want to get in the hands of these curious kids."

"So teaching is a career change for you?" Ryan felt like he'd met a kindred spirit—someone else who had recently made a job shift.

Luke explained how he'd made his way to Port Provident High School and would be moving next year to the new science-and-technology-focused campus when it opened. "And how about you? Have you been with the Foundation long?"

"Only about two months. Before that, I was on the professional poker circuit."

Luke tilted his head slightly. "Lucky Charm?"

Ryan felt a bit taken aback. "I haven't heard that one since March. How'd you know?"

Luke hesitated. It was enough to set Ryan's radar off in a way he hadn't felt since leaving the table at Shamrocks for Students.

"You know Lisa Fleming." Ryan laid it out there.

"We work together." Luke's face lost the relaxed smile he'd had when introducing himself and Philip only moments before.

Ryan needed to know. "Is she planning on being here tonight?"

Luke pointed at a sign near the front of the room. Lisa's headshot took up half the poster. "She's the entertainment."

Ryan couldn't stop staring at the poster. He'd never been sent down the river this swiftly. He'd missed those honey-gold eyes so much. And that smile.

His mouth went dry, just looking at the oversized photograph. What would he do when he called her tomorrow?

He heard footsteps and chatter all around, but none of it broke through.

"Ryan? I'd like to introduce Amanda Marsh, English teacher at Port Provident High. And you already know Lisa Fleming."

"I do." He turned his head away from the photo and toward the reality. "Lisa...it's good to see you."

She had on the black feather dress. He'd seen it almost every night in his dreams for the last two months. Even in a B&B, Lisa looked just as stunning in it as she did under the lights of Vegas. There was nowhere that Lisa wouldn't shine.

"It's surprising to see you, Ryan. Why are you in Port Provident?" Lisa's eyebrows pinched together tightly. She looked fiercely beautiful.

"Work." He gestured around the room.

"But you retired."

"I am now in education, in a manner of speaking."

Lisa stood tall on her shiny, towering heels. "How so?"

"A friend of mine once told me I could make a difference for kids. Tonight's event in partnership with the Cutting Edge Students foundation—they're the ones who run a little St. Patrick's Day poker tournament you attended once upon a time."

She looked around the room. "So you're still playing poker?"

"No, I'm the Director of Development. I'm the bridge between donors and the charity. I'm specifically here tonight to talk with Jake Peoples from the Peoples Family Foundation. Jake and his family have agreed to give the lead gift for the STEM Academy. The building will be named for them."

"Why didn't you tell me?" Her voice dropped to a whisper. It reminded him of bumping into her on the sidewalk beside the pool area at the Renaissance Grand. She'd been scared and angry then.

And he didn't blame her one bit for feeling both of those emotions right now.

"It was a last-minute trip. My boss got sick this morning and needed someone to hop on a plane. I should have called you."

"Yes, you should have."

He heard her loud and clear that time.

He felt some fear of his own as he replied. "I didn't think you wanted to hear from me."

"I never intended for us to not be friends, Ryan. That wasn't what I meant that night in your suite." Lisa picked up a mini quiche from a tray being passed around the room.

Ryan couldn't take his eyes off her. He drank in the sight of her curves in that short black dress like he was still out in the Nevada desert, parched and needing an oasis.

"You were the biggest hand I ever played. I had never met anyone like you. And I didn't want to be just friends. I wanted to give you the fairy tale. We happened in Vegas. And I'd hoped you would stay in Vegas."

Her neck tucked slightly, taking her line of sight away from Ryan's face.

"I couldn't. I'd made commitments. And I couldn't break them. Even if..."

"Even if?" Ryan wanted—no, he needed—her to finish the sentence.

"Even if it broke my heart." She raised her head once again. "But you were right."

"I was?"

"I was wrong. There could have been another way. I should have trusted you enough to talk about it, to find a solution."

Ryan smiled. He had an ace to play. "You want to talk now?"

Lisa's golden eyes darted around the room. "Here? Like this?"

"Why not?" Ryan shrugged. He couldn't keep his smile from growing bigger.

"Because it's a charity fundraiser, not a counseling session?" Skepticism settled across her face.

Ryan put his hands on her shoulders. Feeling the silk of her skin was just as electrifying to him as his days at the top of his game had once been. "A charity fundraiser for your students. The ones you've made a commitment to. Seems like the perfect place to me."

Lisa shook her head, but made no move to shake off his touch. So at least he had that going for him, Ryan thought.

"I have to sing in a moment."

He tugged her a little closer.

"That's okay. This won't take long." Ryan leaned toward Lisa, stopping so his lips were just over her left ear. "I want to go home with the armadillo."

He half expected her to tell him he'd gone crazy. And she'd be right. Crazy for her.

"There's that song again. Amanda was humming it earlier."

"Remember when you told me you weren't going to be my fiancée in Vegas because you wanted to go home?" Ryan stood up straight. He wanted to see Lisa's face clearly in the glow of the candles and twinkle lights that decorated the main event room at the B&B.

She nodded. "Very clearly."

"Well, would you be my fiancée if you could stay home?"

The tiniest of smiles tugged upwards on the corner of her lips. "I don't understand."

"You're home. I'm here. I can now work from anywhere. I could base myself here. With you. What do you think about that?"

Lisa's smile grew. "But what about Nana and Pops?"

Ryan couldn't keep a small laugh from escaping. "Nana's on a beach house kick. She told her doctor she needs to be bi-coastal. She'd move back. And Pops loves to fish."

"If they would come...and you would come..." Lisa trailed off. "Is there anything we've forgotten?"

Ryan nodded and pulled Lisa against him. "Only this."

Leaning down, he kissed her. The regret of the last two months, the one thing that had held him back from throwing himself fully into his new job and his new life melted like snow when confronted with sunshine.

Lisa was his queen, his ace, his biggest jackpot ever.

As he lifted his head, Ryan looked into Lisa's eyes. There was one more thing missing.

"We forgot something else," he said low enough that no one else would hear him.

She didn't move, lingering in the embrace. "What's that?"

"A real proposal. I've asked you to marry me a few times, but those were all practice. This time I mean it." He took both her hands in his. "I don't have a ring—and if I go down on one knee, everyone in here will stare—so I'm going to have to ask you again. But I want to make sure this time you actually give me an answer."

Lisa nodded. "I think that can be arranged."

"Lisa Marie Fleming, will you marry me?"

"Yes." The smile that crossed her face shone brighter than the stars. She snuggled back into his arms, drawing close and lifting her face for another kiss.

"I spent years being the Lucky Charm at the tables, but the day you came into my life, I became lucky in love—and spending forever with you is the greatest jackpot of all."

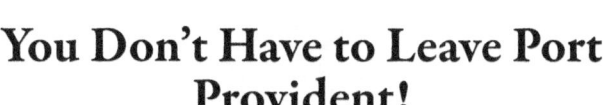

You Don't Have to Leave Port Provident!

Start May I Have This Dance Now!
WHAT IF APRIL SHOWERS COULD BRING MAY SECOND CHANCES?

CLAIR BELL HAS HIDDEN in the shadows for far too long. Depression has haunted her for her entire life, and after a devastating breakup long ago, she knew her heart and mind could never handle hurt like that again. Over the years, she's been able to give her love to the seniors at the retirement community where she works. As she puts together the spring activity calendar, one event visitor puts all her anxieties back in full bloom. Clair can either hold on to the chill that's followed her for years...or accept Rob's apology and allow a second-chance romance to blossom like the May flowers that are returning to Provident Island.

If you love quick, sweet escape romance stories filled with hope, heart, and happily-ever-after that will make you swoon and leave you with a smile, you will want to celebrate the holidays with the residents of the beachside small town of Port Provident.

www.books2read.com/MayIHaveThisDanceBook

Join Kristen's Reader Community Today and Receive a Free Port Provident Story

Join Kristen's reader community today for the latest and get A Place to Find Love, *a sweet escape romance that introduces you to Port Provident, Texas and the residents who find love on the island, for free!*
www.kristenethridge.com/newsletter[1]

---

1. http://www.kristenethridge.com/newsletter

Sneak Peek: May I Have This Dance—Chapter One

"SO, MARTIE, YOU'RE online dating?"

Clair Bell gave the retiree a very puzzled look. Martie Simpson did not seem like the type to swipe left or right...or in any direction, for that matter. In fact, directly over her bed in her studio apartment here at the Port Provident Retirement Community, Martie kept an 11x14 portrait of her being held in her late husband's arms.

Martie laughed. "Oh, Clair, honey, no. I'm just playing games."

Clair didn't realize her eyes could stretch so wide. She could feel the skin in the corners straining to open even larger. "Martie, that's not really smart. The internet is a crazy place. There are so many people who would try to take advantage of you."

"Take advantage of me? Clair, what are you talking about? I'm just playing BuddyWords."

Now Clair felt her eyes narrow until only a mere slit let light in to her pupils. "BuddyWords? The crossword puzzle game?"

Martie's face broke into a grin. "That's the one!"

"So you're playing an online crossword puzzle game and you used it to invite someone to the Valentine dance here at the Retirement Community?"

Clair wanted to understand Martie, she truly did, but this was just downright baffling. When did Martie put down her crochet long enough to learn how to download an app?

"Well, sort of. The person I've been playing with is from here in Port Provident. That's how we started playing together. I met him in the BuddyWords chat room."

Clair clenched her jaw, hoping it would keep her from rolling her eyes. "You met him in the chat room? Okay, so what's his name?"

Martie shrugged. "Bobby0612."

"Martie, that's not a real name. That's a screenname. His last name is not Mr. Oh-Six-One-Two. He could be anyone. He could be a scammer trying to...I don't know...get your Social Security check."

A loud laugh came straight from Martie's throat. "Then he's a dumb scammer. He can have that piddly little thing."

"You know what I mean, though, Martie." Clair found it hard to believe that Martie seemed to think that *Clair* was the crazy one.

"I do." The older woman's gray bun flopped ever-so-slightly on the top of her head as she nodded. "But I've lived long enough wishing for things to be different. I've lived a long time without my Ray. And with my kids away living their own lives in other states, well, I've lived a long time being alone. I'm tired, Clair. You do a great job of planning activities here and making sure we're all looked after. No one could do a better job of running a place like this than you do—there are so many horror stories out there of homes that treat their residents badly. You don't do that, and I know you never will. And I've got friends here—I don't mean that I'm lonely. I just want a little fun. You know?"

Clair raised her arm and patted Martie on the shoulder.

All of Clair's residents had a special home in her heart, but Martie Simpson occupied the penthouse. She loved the dear little woman who was always quoting her favorite Bible verses, telling stories from the war, and gifting hand-made afghan blankets to every new resident. Martie was like the grandmother Clair always dreamed of having.

"I think I do, Martie."

"I know you do, Honey." Martie stared Clair down with love in her gaze. "It wouldn't hurt you to decide to have some fun, too. I said you're great at your job—and you are—but there's a big world outside these walls, you know."

Clair waved at Ellis Lawson as his daughter signed him out for the afternoon. "Be good, Ellis—I'll see you back in a bit."

"See? Even Ellis gets out there. He told me Felicia was taking him to Island Bowl today."

If Clair hadn't known better, she'd say there was more than a hint of *I-told-you-so* in Martie's voice.

"I haven't been bowling since high school." The memories came as swiftly as a shiny ball rolling down the lane. Rob had talked her into joining a league at Island Bowl. He said he was in in it for the chance to have his own monogrammed bowling shirt. He'd always made her laugh.

Until the day that he made her cry.

But that was a long time ago. She had worked hard to stop letting the memories of Rob Landers affect her.

And she didn't intend to change her constant desire to keep the past in the past.

Martie had dragged up enough crazy with this BuddyWords Valentine's date thing. Clair was absolutely not going to let Martie inadvertently pull up anything else that needed to be, metaphorically speaking, left at the bottom of the Gulf of Mexico.

It seemed crazy to lead the conversation back to this BuddyWords nonsense, but it didn't take much for Clair to realize that was a much safer place for her mind to be than dancing around memories of her high school sweetheart.

"So, Mr. Oh-Six-One-Two is going to come here and be your date to the Valentine's Dance we're putting on next weekend?"

Martie shook her head strongly enough that this time, her bun did a full cha-cha. "No, not exactly."

Clair threw her hands in the air. "Then I'm really confused, Martie. I thought that's what you said."

"I did." She nodded again. "But he's also coming tonight to dinner. He's here in town visiting family. It's his first time back in Port Provident in almost ten years, he said."

"He's coming to dinner here? With you?"

Martie smiled. "Yes. It's lasagna night. He said he loves lasagna. It was a bonus word two weeks ago. We started talking about it. I thought it would be fun to meet him in person."

"Martha Jane Sidwell Simpson, you've gone plumb crazy. I think you need a chaperone."

"Nope. There are two hundred and twelve residents here. I'll be fine." She made a dusting motion with her hands as if to signal that was that to Clair. "Now, if you'll excuse me, I need a little beauty nap before dinner."

She gave a grin to Clair, then turned away and walked down the hall without another word.

When Clair told people that she managed activities and recreation for the local retirement center, most of them assumed that her days were spent calling bingo and bocce ball tournaments. They figured it was a slow, sedate job.

They'd never met Martie Simpson. Or the other two hundred and eleven people who called this cluster of red brick buildings near the seashore home.

Nothing about the Port Provident Retirement Community was dull. It was why Clair preferred to spend her time at work. Her own life paled in comparison. Retirees who'd seen everything and done everything still had more excitement in their lives than a woman who had her whole life ahead of her.

She'd be reminded once again of that tonight when she popped in the center's restaurant to check on Martie. Clair wouldn't be on a first date, herself. She never went on first dates. Even though Martie insisted it wasn't a date, Clair could make sure Martie had a good time—and a safe time.

And somehow, Clair would find a way to tell herself that what she had now was enough.

IT FELT GOOD TO BE home.

Rob Landers looked at all the shops and restaurants and other businesses that crowded along the last strip of land before the water—Gulfview Boulevard. So many of them were familiar. Even in the ten years he'd been gone, they'd remained.

He took a deep breath, processing the emotion of seeing his hometown again for the first time in so long. He wished that, like the long-term establishments, he'd been able to stay. But it wasn't meant to be. His old man had needed help and his mom needed a clean break and getting out of town was the only way to make both of those happen.

Still, reconnecting with Port Provident the last few months had done his soul some good. He'd plugged into some groups on FaceSpace online, purchased a digital subscription to the online paper, and even met someone from the island while playing BuddyWords on breaks at work.

He wanted to know if finding his roots could cure the restlessness that had crept under his skin.

If any place could show him the way, it would be Port Provident.

As Rob slowed down at the stop light, he looked to his left, taking in more of the local landscape.

THERE IT WAS. Island Bowl. Man, he'd spent so many hours there. He'd spent so many hours *with Clair* there.

Clair Bell. He'd never forgotten the honey-blonde girl who'd been his first love. But he knew she'd forgotten him. In this whole crazy pursuit of his past, Rob knew without a doubt that the roots that had once connected him to Clair were now shriveled up and dead.

Just like the addiction that chased his pop off the island.

Just like the angry divorce that meant he needed to be separated from his mother and sister.

Just like the freedom and happiness he'd once known while roaming the halls of Port Provident High School.

Just like so many things in his life.

Rob was done with bitter ends and loss.

This trip to Port Provident was about finding himself and giving himself the chance to see how his life could have been different. It was about reconnecting with people and places that had once meant a great deal in his life.

It wasn't about regret. And every memory he had of Clair Bell was wrapped in a cloud of regret. Rob turned his head away from Island Bowl and waited for the light to change from red to green.

Somehow, these few seconds spoke to him deep inside. They were the perfect picture of everything he was trying to do. He was trying not to look at the things in the past that had hurt him—but instead, he was waiting for the sign that he could move forward.

It wasn't long before he saw the sign he'd been looking for—at least for tonight. The Port Provident Retirement Community. He'd met LongTimeMartie online in a forum for people who played an app-based crossword puzzle game called BuddyWords. They struck up a friendship after realizing they had Port Provident in common. When she found out that he was coming to town to see family, she invited him to lasagna night at her retirement home.

His sister Gretel almost laughed herself off the side of her dolphin tour boat when she heard about his plans for dinner.

"She seems like she needs a friend, Gretel. Her daughter just moved to Ohio with her family, but she stayed behind. Now she's all alone on the island. I know what that feels like.

You do too." Rob remembered their conversation from the night before.

"Yeah, I do. I wonder if some knight in shining armor will show up for me when I go to a home someday," Gretel mused.

"I'm no knight. And if I had armor, I'm pretty sure it would be tarnished," Rob told Gretel.

He looked on the passenger seat next to him. He'd bought a dozen roses in a variety of colors. He was no white knight, but he knew that to have a friend, you first had to be a friend. And this trip to Port Provident was all about being a better version of himself and putting together the pieces of the puzzle to help him start over and become who he'd always hoped he could be.

Rob walked in the door to the facility. A tiny woman with a loosely-wound gray bun smiled broadly. "Bobby?"

"LongTimeMartie?"

Her smile became even brighter. He held out the multi-colored blooms. She leaned close and inhaled deeply.

"What a sweet young man you are, Bobby."

He cleared his throat a bit. "I actually go by Rob. Bobby was my nickname when I was a kid. My username is my kid nickname and my birthday. Bobby0612...my birthday's June 12."

"Oh...how cute," the older woman said. "Bet you can't guess how I got mine."

"I'm afraid I can't." There were too many possibilities, and not a one of them seemed like something he wanted to say out loud to a woman old enough to be his grandmother.

Martie took the bouquet from Rob. "It's from my favorite song. *It's Been a Long, Long Time* by Harry James and his Orchestra from back in the World War II days. My husband

and I danced to it the night before he shipped out to Europe. It was our song."

Her explanation brought a smile to his face. "It must be nice to have true love like that."

She closed her eyes. "Oh, it was. I miss him."

"So, he's not here with you?" Rob didn't quite know what else to say.

"Oh, he's always with me," she said, tapping her finger over her heart. "Right in here. Now, let's get to the dining room before Mary Ellen gets the good table. I want to make sure we're sitting right in the center so everyone knows this old girl still has some fun."

CLAIR TRIED TO BE STEALTHY. Although she often worked late and walked around the restaurant area chatting with residents, she felt way too much like a chaperone right now.

Play it cool, Clair Bear. Just play it cool.

Just as she expected, Martie had chosen the table right in the center of the room. It was exactly like her to make sure everyone saw her and that she saw everyone. Martie was hardly ever subtle, and Clair loved her for it.

Everything seemed to be going well. There were two glasses of tea, a basket of bread, two salad plates heaped with spring mix and croutons...and Rob Landers.

Suddenly, nothing was cool.

Everything flipped around like a salad being tossed in a big, wooden bowl.

Why was Martie having dinner with Rob?

Why was Rob even in Port Provident? Clair choked on a little bit of bile. He left. He left in the middle of the night without saying goodbye. He never reached out again. And to her knowledge, he hadn't been back in ten years.

Bobby0612. The twelfth of June. That was his birthday. And his mother used to call him Bobby, even though everyone else called him Rob. Clair wanted to kick herself for not figuring out the user name.

She tried taking a steadying breath, refusing to give into the urge to condemn herself. After all, there were a lot of guys named Bobby in this world. How was she supposed to know that the one who'd broken her heart and actually went by Rob liked to play word games on his phone?

Clair figured all he knew how to do was play mind games.

And heart games.

He'd played her back then. Just like a game.

When Martie's daughter moved up north, Clair promised that she and the rest of the staff would take good care of Martie. And that meant there was no way that she was going to let Rob Landers spend any more time with the retiree. Not even on that silly crossword game. She'd warned Martie about crazy people who wanted to scam retirees out of their life savings.

It wasn't exactly dollars and cents, but Rob had scammed Clair's heart back in high school and run off, leaving it just as empty as any cleaned-out bank account. She knew who Rob Landers was and how he worked, and she was not going to let him anywhere near Martie or any of the other retirees under her watch.

Nope.

Clair was older and wiser. And scared stiff. How could she say anything to Rob after all this time?

She marched across the dining room. She had six more steps to figure it out.

"Martie?" Clair stopped short of the table and crooked her finger. "Can I have a word or two with you for a minute?"

Martie's face lit up like a strand of lights surrounding a Christmas tree. "Of course, darling. But first, I want you to meet my new friend. This is Rob Landers, the real-life Bobby0612. Rob, this is Clair Bell. She's our activities director here. She's like another granddaughter to me."

Clair got a great deal of satisfaction out of watching Rob's complexion drop several shades until it bottomed out somewhere between puke green and ashy gray.

"You work here?"

"This is my home. These are my people." She crossed her arms, hoping to deflect any bad ju-ju that seeing him might stir up. Childish, yes. And the fact that she even so much as thought the words *bad ju-ju* made her roll her eyes at her own ridiculousness. But still...

"Wait, so you live here?"

She stared him down. It was way more fun than it should have been to watch him squirm. "I never left."

"Clair, honey, you sound mad. Do you two know each other?"

"Yes," Rob choked out.

"Not really," Claire said confidently.

Martie laid her fork on the side of her salad bowl. All eyes in the restaurant had turned toward the center table. They'd be talking about this confrontation for days over bingo.

"Clair—do you know him or not?"

Clair decided that honesty was the best policy. "I thought I did. Once. But no, apparently I really didn't."

"So how do you know each other?" Martie continued to dig.

"School." Clair focused on keeping it short.

Unfortunately, Rob had not gotten the same memo. He dove in at the same time as Clair, but gave more of an explanation than she ever wanted her residents to know. "We dated for two years in high school. I haven't seen her since I moved."

Clair stood silent.

"So...you're the one who got away?" Martie began to hum something that sounded suspiciously like a big band tune.

"What are you singing, Martie?"

Martie smiled. "Oh, just my favorite little song. *It's Been a Long, Long Time*."

Clair couldn't even twitch. She was frozen. She knew the lyrics to that song. She did not want Rob to kiss her once or twice or once again. *Never again* seemed far more appropriate.

"It has been a long time," Clair said. She lowered her voice slightly. "But not nearly long enough."

Martie swallowed, then yawned with a big stretch. She pushed the chair back, then stood up. "My goodness, speaking of long, it has been a looong day. And you know what they say about elderly people needing their rest. Rob, I'm so sorry, but I've got to go back to my room. Right now. Really nice meeting you."

For the first time in more than a decade, Clair looked at Rob and saw her own expression mirrored in his dark eyes. The look on his face held the same amount of shock and disbelief as her own features did. Martie scampered out of the room with a rate of speed that belied the number of arthritis pills she took on a daily basis.

Rob took a deep breath and pointed at the now-vacant chair.

"Do you still like lasagna?"

Keep reading May I Have This Dance
Click here: www.books2read.com/MayIHaveThisDanceBook[1]

---

1. http://www.books2read.com/MayIHaveThisDanceBook

The Holiday Hearts Series

The Right Resolution[1]
The Cupid Caper[2]
Lucky in Love[3]
May I Have This Dance[4]
First Kiss Fireworks[5]
Falling Forever This Time[6]
Thankful for Love[7]
Mission: Mistletoe[8]

Want to extend your stay in Port Provident?
Start reading the Hearts and Hope Series

Shelter from the Storm[9]
The Doctor's Unexpected Family[10]
His Texas Princess[11]

---

1. http://www.books2read.com/TheRightResolutionBook

2. http://www.books2read.com/TheCupidCaperBook

3. http://www.books2read.com/LuckyInLoveBook

4. http://www.books2read.com/MayIHaveThisDanceBook

5. http://www.books2read.com/FirstKissFireworksBook

6. http://www.books2read.com/FallingForeverThisTimeBook

7. http://www.books2read.com/ThankfulForLoveBook

8. http://www.books2read.com/MissionMistletoeBook

9. http://www.books2read.com/ShelterFromTheStorm

10. http://www.books2read.com/TheDoctorsUnexpectedFamily

Holiday of Hope[12]

Other Books by Kristen

Love Hallmark movies? Pick up Kristen's book October Kiss, based on the Hallmark movie viewers love! Available anywhere books are sold—in paperback, digital, and audio! October Kiss from Hallmark Publishing[13]

---

11. http://www.books2read.com/HisTexasPrincess

12. http://www.books2read.com/HolidayOfHope

13. https://www.books2read.com/OctoberKiss

About Kristen

KRISTEN ETHRIDGE WRITES Sweet Escape Romance—stories with hope, heart and happily-ever-after—for Harlequin's Love Inspired line, Hallmark Publishing, and Laurel Lock Publishing. She's a Romance Writers of America Golden Heart Award nominee and both a Christian Fiction and Inspirational Romance #1 Best-Selling Author.

You can find Kristen in her native habitat—a Texas patio—where she's likely to be savoring the joy of a crispy taco, along with a glass of iced tea. Scents from her essential oil diffuser are also a must, since she's a certified aromatherapist. She's almost convinced her family that it's normal to talk to imaginary people, as long it goes in a book.

Find her online at http://www.kristenethridge.com where you can get a free story for signing up for her newsletter. You can also follow her adventures in writing at www.facebook.com/kristenethridgebooks[1].

Keep up with Kristen by joining her newsletter list[2] and her author pages on Bookbub[3] and Facebook[4]. If you can't get enough of Port Provident, come join the Port Provident Community Center[5] on Facebook, the official gathering place for Kristen and her fans.

www.kristenethridge.com[6]

Facebook[7] Instagram[8]

The Port Provident Community[9] Center

Don't forget...if you love sweet escape romances, join Kristen's newsletter[10]!

1.   http://www.facebook.com/kristenethridgebooks

2.   http://www.kristenethridge.com/newsletter

3.   https://www.bookbub.com/authors/kristen-ethridge

4.   http://www.facebook.com/kristenethridgebooks

5.   https://www.facebook.com/groups/2422381554654795

6. http://www.kristenethridge.com

7. https://www.facebook.com/KristenEthridgeBooks

8. https://instagram.com/kristenethridge

9. https://www.facebook.com/groups/2422381554654795

10. http://www.kristenethridge.com

Acknowledgements

TO MY FANTASTIC BOSS, Angelia...who had the brilliant idea to drag me along on that trip to Las Vegas and made sure I had dinner at the Venetian...aka the Renaissance Grand.

LAUREL LOCK PUBLISHING

Publisher's Note: This is a work of fiction. Names, characters, places, and incidents are a product of the author's imagination. Locales and public names are sometimes used for atmospheric purposes. Any resemblance to actual people, living or dead, or to businesses, companies, events, institutions, or locales is completely coincidental.

Scriptures taken from the Holy Bible, New International Version®, NIV®. Copyright © 1973, 1978, 1984, 2011 by Biblica, Inc.™ Used by permission of Zondervan. All rights reserved worldwide. www.zondervan.com[1] The "NIV" and "New International Version" are trademarks registered in the United States Patent and Trademark Office by Biblica, Inc.™

Book Layout ©2013 BookDesignTemplates.com

1.   http://www.zondervan.com/